TEA AT THE OPALACO

and other stories

Jane Lockyer Willis

TSL Publications

First published in Great Britain in 2016
By TSL Publications, Rickmansworth

ISBN / 978-1-911070-23-8

DEDICATION

To Ron Nicol
who has helped and supported me
with my play writing.

CONTENTS

TEA AT THE OPALACO

'It was quite awful!' The slight curl of the lip, the half-smile of despair. 'I forgot he was coming, you see. I must have looked a complete clown with cream smeared all over my mouth. And Ralph catching me like that. Too awful!'

She waves a heavily ringed hand over the deep cushioned sofas, at the waiters: conciliatory, charming, serving tea at occasional tables set with white cloths and silver cutlery.

Sitting in the corner, an American couple. They nod, smile. I smile back - a nervous, wish I weren't here sort of smile.

'So, what did you do?' My eyes once more fixed on Jesse.

'I re-ordered.'

'For Ralph?'

'For both of us.'

'A full afternoon tea for the two of you? Are you serious?'

'I have just said so, Helen. In any case, teas at the Opalaco are decidedly paltry compared with other places. And how could Ralph enjoy his food with me sitting there watching every mouthful?'

She takes her napkin and wipes her mouth a lip at a time. 'It would have embarrassed him had I not done so. It was the least I could do.'

Latria homage to this man, thirty years her junior with whom she plans to share her worldly goods.

I glance again at the Americans - at the windows - fabric heavy, at the pale panelled walls, the chandeliers. The golds, the reds and the greens; trademarks of absolute luxury. Now back to Jessie - peevish, bored - waving her teaspoon at the waiter to attract attention.

'A bottle of *Dom Perignon*, please, and three glasses.'

I am about to ask why three glasses when I notice the waiter's eyes fix on the spoon.

'Have you finished with that, madam?'

She looks at him: half smiles, allows it to drop into the saucer.

'Yes, thank you.'

'Thank *you*, madam.'

And now he stacks the tray with our dirty plates, cups, saucers and the one remaining raspberry tart.

'Who is the extra glass for Jessie?' I ask.

'For Ralph.'

'Ralph? Is Ralph coming here?'

'It's time you met him, Helen.'

'You never said he was coming.'

'Didn't I?' Her gaze falters. She reaches for her handbag, fingers fumbling with the clasp. I notice her hands tremble slightly as she dabs loose powder on highly pinked cheeks then lipsticks a mouth plump, impatient and wanting.

I sigh. Her insolence leaves me little room to breathe. I am hers for the duration of the day.

The Americans are leaving now. The waiter offers to have their packages sent ahead to their suite: carrier bags bearing the names, *Harrods, Burberry, Dickens and Jones.*

'There is just one thing.' Jessie snaps shut the snake skin bag.

'Yes?'

'I should warn you.'

'What about?'

'Ralph.'

'Oh?'

'He may not be quite what you're expecting.' She stops. Glares. The Americans are walking over to us.

'Pardon me for intruding.' The woman's eyes, candid and kind meet mine. Her scent is light and lemony. 'I've been admiring that beautiful scarf of yours.'

'Oh. Thank you.' I take the large silk square from around my shoulders, studying it as though for the first time.

'Was it made in England?'

'Italy, I think. It was a present.' And as I hand it to her, her well manicured hands touch it with such gentleness I feel almost soothed, stroked, relaxed.

'The colours! Look Bill. Those reds and greens. So rich, so vivid.'

He nods, gives me a broad-mouthed grin. 'Real pretty, ma'am.'

'Are you here on holiday?' I want to detain them, to share their mood: light, airy, and fun.

'We are. Bill and I are touring London then next week, we hope to visit your Stratford-Upon-Avon.'

Our champagne arrives and Jessie makes an audible fuss. Is it cold enough? And nuts, where are the nuts?

'Won't you both join us?' The words out before I can stop myself. I blush. Dare not look at Jessie: feel her stare, her cold disapproval.

'Well, that is so kind.' The woman turns to her husband.

'We don't drink, thank you,' he says, his arm around her waist. 'But we'd love to chat awhile, if that's okay with you. We've only got to walk the length of the corridor for our dinner. Eating early tonight. We're going to see *Les Miserables*. Oh, pardon me. I'm forgetting my manners. I'm Bill and this is my wife, Sue.'

Introductions over I ask them to sit down.

'Wonderful sofas.' Sue, resting her ash-blonde head against the back, and half-closing her eyes, 'You could just sink into them and not move for a week.'

The talk is of New York, London and The Cotswolds. Jessie sits tight lipped, barely attending, frequently directing her glance towards the entrance: her eyes, light coloured beads tucked into dimpled flesh.

'You waiting for someone?' Bill asks her.

'My fiancé.'

'Well, congratulations!'

Jessie smiles: that amused curling of the lips that I remember so well - that mischievous, challenge me if you dare, quirk. Here again was the girl who all those years back, had befriended me at St Agnes School, who introduced me to her gang, chose me for the hockey team, and invited me home for tea once a week.

Looking back, I think that Jessie saw me as a kind of challenge. I was the interloper, the pupil who arrived late on in the fourth form, the girl she chose to adopt and integrate into school society. Bossy, adventurous Jessie took me under her wing. Being her friend demanded a certain compliance on my part but by nature I was obedient and the rewards meant automatic entry into her circle: the elite few who inspired envy and praise from the less intrepid, the less impetuous class members. I realise now that I cruised on her back far too long, my eternal gratitude stifling independence, that unrestrained freedom for which I should have readily fought.

As a young woman, Jesse was beautiful with strong auburn hair and eyes the colour of green Chartreuse. Men were a little in awe of her: her arrogance, her impetuous nature. But Jessie's looks, her sex appeal enticed those brave enough to challenge her restless needs, and a few proposed marriage.

But Jessie wanted to become an actress, had all the requisites: an outgoing personality, coquetish charm and stage presence. But then she had an accident - fell from her horse and broke her leg in two places. After that things changed. She was left with a slight limp, ceased riding, and gave up any idea of going into the theatre. The slim, lithe girl became fat and discontented.

She later married Terence, a giant among industrialists, who spent most of their long marriage amassing money and playing golf. I would listen tirelessly to accounts of his unfaithfulness coupled with her own affairs: little intrigues that always ended on a furious note. As the years went by, Jessie grew increasingly self-centred, angry and resentful. Her binges, her diets, were frequent, but her discontent and boredom with life tended to fuel her hunger and her weight ballooned. Embittered by her 'lost life', as she called it, she developed the art of the one liner, the put down, the pay back.

When Terence died of a heart attack, he left her with an ugly country house near Warwick and a good deal of cash. Although plump her face still retained some of its prettiness and men continued to find her attractive. But single again, many of her women friends saw her as a threat and using the excuse that they were sick of her sharp tongue and scathing manner soon dropped her.

She began spending time at her Belgravia flat: visiting the theatre, museums and hotels for something to do, somewhere to go. In the mornings, a museum and then on to a hotel for lunch or tea. Occasionally, like today, she would take me with her. Jessie had met Ralph at *Browns*. I knew little about him apart from his youth. Jessie could be secretive at times, telling me only what she wanted me to hear and I was surprised when their friendship developed and they became engaged.

'Where is Ralph? He's so late.' Jessie pouring herself another glass of champagne while Sue and Bill make encouraging noises, jogging us along with stories about their own lateness.

I am beginning to wish that they would go. Their conviviality is starting to get on my nerves. This consociation grasped so eagerly a few minutes earlier has chilled in the wake of Jessie's increasing agitation. There is something out of alignment here, yet I can't put my finger on it.

'Jessie,' I say, at length, 'why don't you telephone Ralph?'

'No!'

'But why not?'

'Because his club doesn't take kindly to women friends calling. If he doesn't show up soon, we'll go.'

A small group of guests wander into the lounge and order drinks from the bar. Their arrival jolt Bill and Sue into action and they prepare to leave. There are promises of future contacts, the exchange of address cards, goodbyes, some consorting with the staff, a wave, and they are gone.

'What dreadful people,' says Jessie, draining her glass. 'I really don't know why you had to encourage them Helen.'

I am to feel guilty now and for a while we sit in moody silence.

'Shall we go?' she says at length, pencilled eyebrows raised.

I nod, thankful to be leaving at last, and Jessie summons the waiter who helps her into her mink coat. There is no further mention of Ralph as we walk out of the lounge, through reception and onto the street. Her bearing is stately, even with the slight limp she reminds me of a queen embarking on her coronation.

The doorman summons a taxi, and I wave her off - watch, as it circles the square, before heading for Park Lane and the mid-week traffic.

An early evening drizzle coupled with a cold north westerly wind whips the leaves from their trees, driving them into gutters and around my feet. I shiver. Another late autumn. Hugging my coat around me I suddenly realise that I have forgotten my headscarf.

I go back inside. It is still there, the scarf, on the small table where I had left it. A family of four are now sitting in our former places sipping glasses of red wine.

'Excuse me, madam.' The maitre d'hotel hurries towards me. 'May I have a word?'

'Of course.'

He draws me aside. 'Now that you are alone, I feel it necessary to speak my mind.' His tone is quiet, reverent almost.

'Yes?'

'It concerns your friend.'

'Mrs Lacey?'

'Mrs Lacey. Yes. It is something of a delicate nature.' The hand to the mouth, the small cough. 'As you are probably aware, she visits our hotel from time to time.'

'Yes, she likes The Opalaco - enjoys the teas here.'

He pauses, gives the faintest of bows. 'Indeed, she does.'

'So, what was it you wanted to discuss?'

A pause and then: 'Mrs Lacey has been taking things.'

'Taking things?'

'Stealing.'

'Oh!'

'Teaspoons, the odd pastry fork and knife.'

'Surely not.'

'I'm afraid so.'

I am at a loss. 'But today. She didn't take anything today?'

'No, madam. Not today.'

'She probably doesn't realise what she's doing. Mrs Lacey can be forgetful, admits it herself. Only this afternoon she was telling me …'

'It's not unusual for elderly people such as herself, to be a little careless, that is true.'

'I said forgetful. That is not quite the same, surely.'

And when he does not answer, 'You have proof of her taking things?'

He inclines his head. A discreet admittance. Poor, poor Jessie.

'The point that I wish to make madam, is that it might only be a matter of time before she steps it up.'

'Steps it up? What do you mean?'

'We value our customers. I'm sure you will understand that any level of theft has to be taken seriously.'

'She might steal from the guests? Is that what you're implying?'

'Possibly. Given time. It would be advisable therefore, a kindness, if you were to tell her - discreet as I am sure you will be, not to return to The Opalaco.'

'But I can't. I can't stop her. She wouldn't listen to me.'

Then it was only fair to warn me that should Mrs Lacey insist on coming back, she would not be made welcome. His emphasis on the word *not*, leaves me in little doubt as to what might happen should she do so.

He bids me good night and turns away. Now issues an instruction to a waiter: the one who had served us tea. A few moments later, the young man passes me carrying a tray of drinks. His face reddens. He does not acknowledge me.

Two days slip by. The winds are still high and some of the slates are off my roof. A garden statue of a young girl holding a basket of fruit has smashed on my patio. I am not normally superstitious but I cannot help wondering if this might be portentous in some way.

I have still not rung Jessie about the 'delicate' issue. How to approach this rich, proud old friend? My timidity, life-long: my faint heartedness, my desire to please, resists confrontation of any kind. She is bound to be furious that the maitre d'hotel should have spoken about her behind her back. And to me.

I stand by the phone building my courage, idly skimming through a travel brochure half-promising myself that I should take a break: a proper holiday. But not yet. Not after what has happened. Jessie's distress over her forgetfulness with Ralph, coupled with his failure to show up the other afternoon, not to mention the cutlery incident ... Oh, dear, is she growing senile? Have I been ignoring her cries for help?

The telephone rings. I startle to hear Jessie's voice excited, tense. She is on a diet, she tells me. Another one? Yes, but this time she means to stick to it. And darling, she hopes I won't mind, but there are to be no more tea outings for the present, no more visits to the London hotels for cakes and scones and champagne. This time she is firm in her resolve. And when I ask her what has brought this on, she mentions the name William. William? A retired judge who has just moved into the downstairs flat. They met by chance in the lift two days ago. He was dressed in running shorts and was on his way to Green Park for his daily jog. They got chatting and he suggested a walk sometime and then on somewhere for a drink. And look at the size of her! Rather flattering to be asked though, didn't I think?

Jessie's caprices I am used to but Ralph. What about Ralph? I insist.

She pauses long enough to light a cigarette - always keeps a packet by the telephone.

'I rang when I got home,' she says finally.

'And?'

'They told me he was in bed with a chill.'

'They? Who are they, Jessie?'

A catch of the breath. A sigh.

'Well?'

'The staff.'

'The staff at his club?'

Another pause.

'Ralph lives in a home.'

'What sort of a home?'

'A retirement home.'

'But you said he was young.'

'I know I did.'

'That he was thirty years younger than you.'

'Look, Helen. I was going to tell you the other afternoon but then those frightful Americans stuck their noses in and the moment was lost.'

Silence while I try to take this in.

'I was going to tell you Helen. I was. Anyway, Ralph's young in spirit and that's what counts. And it was his choice.'

'What was?'

'To sell his house. To move. He said he was finding the stairs too much of a climb. They have lifts in the other place. I think he has a minor heart complaint but nothing serious.'

'And where is this home Jesse?'

'Just round the corner from The Opalaco.'

'I see.'

'He can come and go as he pleases.' A dry laugh. 'We always referred to it as the club, you know. To say you live in a home sounds so over the hill, so defeatist, so worn out, don't you think?'

I close my eyes. The club. Of course!

'Are you still there? Helen?'

'Yes. I'm still here.'

'We used to play dares. Silly, I know. But it put a bit of spice into our lives: a bit of grit.' Another chuckle. 'It was Ralph who dared me to eat all that tea at The Opalaco. I was very nearly sick but I did it. I jolly well did it.'

'But you'd forgotten he was coming that time. That's what you told me when we were having tea the other day. You'd been distressed because he turned up and you'd forgotten all about it. That's what you said. You were quite upset.'

'I know, I know. I shouldn't have led you on. It was naughty. But he and I, we played games, you see, dares. They were like little plays, sketches. That afternoon, the one I told you about, I'd gone to The Opalaco and ordered tea, just for myself. That was the plan you see. And then half an hour later just as I was tucking into the last fairy cake on the plate, he arrived. I threw up my hands in horror pretending I'd forgotten he was coming. And so then I insisted on re-ordering afternoon tea for the two of us. And I ate mine all over again. I fairly stuffed myself. Ralph and I acted all this up to the hilt. Cramming the food into our mouths as though we hadn't eaten for a week. It was screamingly funny. You should have seen the looks on the waiters' faces. And as for the guests - well! I'm sure they all thought we were bonkers.'

'And your engagement?'

'Oh, that was to get back at those one-time friends of mine. The thought of fat Jessie having a toy boy! They'd be insanely jealous. No, Ralph was just a mate.' Already speaking of him in the past tense.

'And how old is Ralph?'

'Oh, I don't know.'

'How *old*, Jessie?'

'Eighty-two. And there's no need to shout.'

'You lied to me.'

'Just a bit of fun. Just a tease that's all.'

'Was it Ralph who dared you to steal the cutlery?'

'You know about that? How do you know about that?'

'The maitre d'hotel. He told me.'

'Oh did he now! Hah! We knew what we were doing, you know.'

'I've no doubt that you did.'

She giggles. 'We knew that we might be turned out. But that was half the fun, you see. We may be old but we're not old fools. Ralph and I were careful to choose the hotels we liked least in which to play our pranks, although I must say that I did enjoy The Opalaco rather more than most. That's why I returned. Such nerve! And his 'club' so close.'

'So, let me get this straight, Jessie. That fiasco with the tea, Ralph's age, his address and your engagement - all a pretence?'

'You really do love itemising, don't you, Helen? At school, you were always making lists.'

'Answer me.'

'Yes, all a pretence. Games can become addictive, you know.'

'No, I didn't know. But do tell me.'

'At first it's just the two of you: a private little entertainment, a shared diversion. But sometimes the games take hold: you start believing in them. Sometimes others ...'

'Get caught in the cross-fire?'

'I don't know why you're so angry Helen. Too sensitive by half, that's your trouble.'

'Oh, really?'

'Yes, you always were. Even at school I had to protect your back, save you from yourself. You were always such a serious little thing. You know, you really should go out more, stop brooding at home so much. Have some fun.'

My throat aches with rage.

'You used me, Jessie.'

'What?'

'I was there for you and you used me.'

'Listen to me Helen. When you grow old and bored: when you don't play bridge or whist, long for time to pass but hate your afternoon nap, you'll do anything for a bit of a lift, a bit of a buzz.'

'Is that so! Well, shall I tell you what I did for my lift, for my buzz?'

'If you must, but there's really no need …'

'I spent time in the company of a woman who prefers the luxury of pretence to the honest companionship of an old friend.'

I put down the phone. Trembling, I pick up the travel brochure, walk to the sideboard and pour myself a large glass of sherry. I sit, drink, thumb angrily through the pages: Italy, Spain, France, Austria. The Seychelles. I pause. 'A holiday to remember,' it says. 'Meet new friends. Enjoy the nightlife. Spoil yourself rotten! Book now and expect a twenty per cent discount.'

I make a note of the number, pour myself another sherry then dial.

I am going to The Seychelles.

LETTUCE AND LETTICE

Sally sampled her first lettuce at the age of five. Salad was one of the few things she would eat. That she grew up at all was a minor miracle as she ate so little. But she did and at the age of twelve was sent to an expensive boarding school on the English coast where on school outings, limp lettuce sandwiches were issued to each pupil. Most girls threw theirs away, but because Sally liked lettuce, she ate hers all up. Despite the large termly fees, meals were scant and almost Dickensian in quantity and quality. The tuck shop did for them, sustaining over the years, an unhealthy crop of pimples caused by an overdose of sugar.

In the upper third, Sally sat next to a girl called Lettice Grudge. She was heavy and wide and their thighs touched as they sat squashed together behind the double desk they shared. Elbows bumped, handwriting jogged and tempers flared, as they silently fought for territorial rights, grappling with pens and push. Lettice wore glasses and a brace and her breath smelt of onions. The two girls avoided each other at playtime. It was not done to be seen with Lettice Grudge. Her name alone invited derision but undaunted and resourceful by nature, she made friends with a girl from the form below.

Lettice shone at Religious Studies and Elocution. With her clear and expressive voice, she was often picked to read aloud in class, passages from *Jane Eyre, Wuthering Heights* and the Bible.

Years later and Sally married Dan. Dan came as a package: one church, one country parish, one ugly brick vicarage and one overgrown garden. Sally could not see herself as vicar's wife material. But Dan was set on having her and love got in the way, so that was that. Oh well! If the going got tough, there was always food to fall back on.

The parish of Long Fittbourne proved every bit as busy as she'd predicted. And now there were snacks to wake up to, to come home to and to go to bed with.

'I need to eat,' she told Dan as he watched her pile a large helping of chocolate soufflé and double cream onto her plate. 'It's all this nervous energy I use up helping you with your parishioners,' she scowled. All this sugar was making her irritable. At night, Dan picked out the crumbs that rolled onto his side of the bed. He said nothing.

And then one Sunday the dam burst!

'I can't cope!' she yelled, throwing his newly ironed surplice into his freshly shaven face. 'I've no time to call my own. I run this monstrous house for you and run myself ragged in the village. I am nothing more than your unpaid secretary. I want out!'

'Out?' He looked alarmed.

'If you don't get a curate to help you, I'm leaving.'

'Leaving?' His firm mouth dropped open.

'That's what I said. Leaving!'

There was a moment's pause and then, 'I understand, darling.'

He did? Wasn't he going to stop her? A wave of panic swept through Sally.

'I've been expecting too much of you,' he said, putting his arms around her. 'I'm sorry. You're quite right to be cross with me. I'll have a word with the bishop and see what can be done. Of course, it will depend on diocesan funds and availability. But I promise to try.'

Sally dried her eyes, reached for the sugar bowl and popped two lumps of soothing sweetness into her mouth. She wished that she'd spoken up sooner. It had really been quite easy after all and with a promise of success.

Dan put on his cassock in readiness for morning service.

How does he keep so thin, she thought, as she heaved her bulk out of the kitchen chair. And how could she stop these awful hunger pangs? Her brain nudged her stomach umpteen times a day: a Mars Bar here, a tub of ice-cream there. And why didn't Dan say something! Shout, scream, anything but something! Too blooming holy! I bet he was a goody goody at school. Teacher's pet, I bet!

Sometimes she caught Dan looking at her - a sad, weary look that filled her with a mixture of irritation and fear. Oh well! I have every excuse, being stuck in the middle of nowhere, being Christian twenty-four hours a day. It's lucky for him that I haven't taken to drink. She turned on the television to drown the sound of the church bells.

'No church for me today,' she shouted, retrieving a half-eaten Crunchie Bar from behind a cushion. 'I am on strike!'

Dan asked the bishop and the bishop said yes, and two male prospective curates visited Long Fittbourne to look and to be looked at. One said it was too big, the other too small. Dan liked one but not the other, so that was the end of that until one bright Saturday in October.

It was Sally's turn to do the church flowers, a job she detested, not least because they made her sneeze. She was by the lectern, attempting to arrange a bunch of straggly hydrangeas rescued from among the many various weeds that carpeted the vicarage garden.

The church clock struck eleven. Her stomach rumbled bang on cue demanding its mid-morning fix - coffee and that large doughnut she'd squirreled away behind the microwave. Yes, she was hiding food now.

'Oh that will do. I'm off!' This said just as Dan entered through the vestry door. Following him was a young blonde woman, tall, willowy and very attractive. Who was this?

Feeling like the Michelin man, she wiped her hands on her none too clean apron, switched on her official smile and went over to join them.

'This is Sally, my wife,' said Dan. He was positively sparkling. 'Darling, this is Letitia.'

They shook hands. Hers was firm and confident, Sally's was damp and soiled. 'Letitia may be coming to work with us,' Dan went on, his round face beaming.

Sally's face froze. Not a woman! Not a blonde bomb shell of a curate.

'I'm about to show Letitia round the church,' said Dan, one hand supporting her elbow.

Hands off! Sally's radar was working overtime.

'And what a beautiful church it is,' enthused Letitia, casting her long lashed eyes round the Norman building with their barrel arches and stone sculptured pulpit.

'Well, I'll leave you two to it,' quipped Sally with a tight nervous laugh. She thought there was something vaguely familiar about the woman. Now what was it?

Weaving her way between the gravestones, the short cut back to the vicarage, she wracked her brains. Where had she seen her before? The WI? The Mother's Union? Prayer meeting? No, no, no. Sunday school outing? Egg and spoon race? Bible study? No! This woman wasn't local, and yet ...

As Sally tucked into her morning break, the plump sugary doughnut did little to satisfy her misgivings. She was beginning to wish she hadn't complained to Dan about her work load. Although she'd never dream of telling him so, she'd rather work her fingers to the bone than risk losing her husband to a gorgeous looking creature like that. Oh come on! She rinsed her cup under the cold tap; Dan would never be unfaithful to her. She trusted him. Didn't she? Sally reached for the biscuit tin.

Letitia's induction to the parish was attended by a large congregation all eager to see what their new female curate was like. Even dressed in a plain cassock and surplice she managed to look good, and her pleasant outgoing manner, everyone agreed, would be an asset to the parish and help swell diminishing congregations.

Meanwhile, Sally attempted to hide her ever increasing weight under even bigger skirts and blouses, and her envy behind even broader smiles.

How dare Letitia reveal her shapely size twelve figure in those close fitting suits! Even the dog collar she wore seemed to add to her allure. And she wasn't just looks either. Letitia turned out some pretty gritty sermons. Made you think, they did. And she had a lovely reading voice, blast her! Yes, thought Sally one Sunday, as she closed her eyes to listen to her reading one of the lessons. This woman has poise. This woman has class. But where, oh where had she met her before?

And then, just as the mellifluous tones washed over her, it suddenly dawned. Her eyes shot open. Lettice Grudge! Top in Religious Studies and Elocution.

Sally stared transfixed. Was it possible? This perfectly coifed, slim creature standing behind the brass eagled lectern, holding every member of the congregation enrapt? This ugly duckling, the girl they had loved to mock, grown into this beautiful swan? Shame faced, Sally glanced down at her own podgy hands clasped tightly in her lap. How things came back to haunt you! Once thin, *she* was now fat. And Letitia, once fat, was now thin!

The woman standing up there, her head erect, was happy, good natured and comfortable in her own skin, while Sally was unhappy, bad tempered and anything but comfortable in hers. If she wasn't careful, didn't take a grip on herself, she would lose self respect all together and what was worse, she could lose Dan's.

The final hymn was *Onward Christian Soldiers*. Right! thought Sally. Action!

'I know who you are!' she blurted after the service. 'You're Lettice Grudge. We shared a desk in the upper third.'

Letitia looked at her with steady blue eyes.

'That's right,' she said.

Well, that's taken the wind out of my sail, thought Sally and felt herself redden. But before she could think of an answer, Letitia went on:

'I knew who *you* were, Sally. Your face hadn't changed that much, but I wasn't sure that you'd want to know who *I* was. So I kept quiet. I changed my name to Letitia. Lettice made me feel like a blooming vegetable.'

They stared at one another in silence, remembering the past, the jibes, the pain, the fun poking. Sally could feel every muscle in her body tense. What to do now? But she needn't have worried. She let out a long sigh of relief when Letitia held out her hand.

'Friends?'

'Friends,' said Sally and they hugged one another and laughed.

'Is that why you changed your surname as well as your Christian name?' Sally asked.

'Yes. I removed the G. Simple really. Letitia Rudge sounds much better than Lettice Grudge, don't you think? Now I don't feel like a resentful lettuce!'

'You certainly don't look like one. You look terrific!' And Sally meant every word. The past would never be forgotten, but forgiven? She hoped so.

'Fancy a coffee one day next week?' said Sally, walking with her to the vestry door.

'Thanks. I'd like that.'

Sally felt more positive, the most positive she'd felt in a long time. She had made a friend and no longer felt threatened. She felt … now, how did she feel? Empowered - Yes, that was the word. Here was someone who had fought against all odds and come out on top. Well, if Letitia could do it then so could she. Things were about to change. She would lose some weight. No more bingeing on chocolate, doughnuts, or slices of pizza. No more complaining, no more envy or lame excuses. Self discipline! That was the thing. There was help at hand too - weight watchers, diet sheets, a local keep fit club, plus a new hairdressers that had opened in the village.

And as for Dan well, he was about to see a change in her too. A change for the better.

OVER BUTTERED SCONES

I stare - gaze horrified at the thick, red stain bleeding onto the tablecloth.

Has she noticed, the woman who just passed me the strawberry preserve? And the man on my right, stirring his tea, spoon clanking the sides of his cup - did he see?

I stare ahead - dare not risk the glint of amusement, the disdain, the disapproval. Newcomer that I am.

On the table opposite, a girl of around nine or ten slides around on her seat, lifts the sides of the table cloth and makes faces. Taking the teaspoon from her mother's cup she now places it under the cloth. Next, she steals the tea knife from the young man next to her. He does not see being deep in conversation with his neighbour. She scrambles under the table with it. Her mother chatting to a woman two places on also does not see.

The scone sits on my plate untouched. I try not to dwell on the stain but I keep noticing it out the corner of my eye: large and disrepute. No-one ever told me how to cope with spilt jam on tablecloths. I had been taught to say please and thank you and enquire after a person's health. I had been brought up to sit up straight, to refrain from placing elbows on tables and not to burp. But as to spillages, I knew nothing. I do remember though my mother saying that if I were to accidentally drop my table napkin in a restaurant, I should leave it for the waiter to pick up. Perhaps in that case, I should alert the waitress next time she came round to re-fill our cups.

'I'm awfully sorry, I really am, but I spilt jam on the table cloth.'

Would she feel obliged to replace it with a clean one? Would she lose her job if she didn't? All those plates, cups, saucers, knives, pastry forks, scones, sandwiches and cakes, would all have to be removed leaving the guests at our table high and dry with nothing to do?

If they had nothing to do what would they do?

Perhaps they would secretly price each other's shoes, or visit other tables and chat about this and that. Or they may feel obliged to hang about, eyes focused on the entrance as though waiting for a train. They might stand on tip-toe and wave to friends across the large marble pillared room; or they might simply stare into space.

'Would you pass the cup cakes please? I can't quite reach.'

An elderly man sitting on my right has his eyes fixed on the multi-coloured dainties placed on a silver platter.

I nod, lift it, offer it to him with a smile that doesn't quite reach my eyes. He takes the one covered in thick pink icing with a cherry on the top.

'I love cake,' he says, taking a large bite. 'I could eat cake all day. But my waistline, you know.' He pats his corpulent tummy. 'My favourites are jam doughnuts.'

At mention of the word jam, I suddenly have an idea. Without thinking twice and in one smart move, I pick up the tray again and place it over the stain. It covers it beautifully. I sit back. Sigh with relief. Why on earth hadn't I thought of that before?

'Why did you do that?' the man asks, spluttering crumbs over the table.

'No reason,' I say, feeling hot with daring.

'Do you like things to be arranged in straight lines?'

'I beg your pardon?'

'You've just created a line segment bounded by two distinct end points.'

'Have I?'

'There's the plate of cup cakes, here's a plate of rather good cucumber sandwiches, and here is a plate of delicious currant scones. All in a perfectly formed line which you have helped create.'

His breath smells of strong peppermints as he lowers his voice, and leans towards me.

'Do tell me. Are you one of those people who avoid treading on the cracks of pavements?'

I am about to say that I am not, when a commotion at the table opposite stops both of us in our tracks. The young girl has re-emerged from under the table, knife in hand and is being harangued by the young man sitting next to her. He has taken off his suede shoes and is waving them plus bits of shoelaces in the air.

'Look what she's done everyone! Look what that wretched girl's done to my shoe laces. Shred them to bits. How am I to get home without shoe laces?'

He turns to the girl's mother. 'You should teach your daughter to behave herself. Spoilt brat!'

At the mention of the word 'brat', the mother shoots to her feet and begins screaming abuse at him, her gold loop earrings swinging back and forth. The girl darts once more under the table, taking half the cloth with her. The manager is called.

Guests stir and start to leave. They are not used to such scenes. Literary lunches are more their style. Children are banned from those. This tea is a one off.

I rise and begin collecting my things.

'I do admire your courage,' says the woman who had passed me the strawberry preserve.

I look at her with amazement.

'You remained so calm,' she says, picking up her handbag and arranging her chiffon scarf.

'Calm?'

'When you spilt the jam. I would have flapped and made a complete fool of myself. But you sat it out; never moved a muscle. I think that's splendid.'

She pats my hand before gliding off, her silver silk jacket draped casually over slim shoulders.

Had she meant it, or was she being sarcastic? But no, her frank blue eyes, her rich warm tone seemed genuine enough.

I am walking on air. You can never tell how things will turn out.

On my way out, I spot the young girl standing at the entrance with her mother. They are waiting for a taxi; mother busy on her mobile, daughter drawing gum from her mouth in one long strip. Buoyed now with my recovered confidence, I go up to her.

'How on earth did you manage to remove that man's shoe-laces and cut them up without his noticing?' I ask.

The mother looks at me in amazement. 'He did notice. And didn't we know about it,' she fumes, her earrings on the move again.

'Only after I'd cut them into little bits,' the girl says, hopping from one foot to the other.

'So, how did you do it?' I persist.

'Easy as a pie. He was gassing away, he didn't even notice. Byes!'

And she's off, whizzing through the swing doors, her mother screaming for her to wait.

On my way to the underground, I bump into the elderly man who had sat on my right. He appears breathless, concentrating with furrowed brow on steering his shabby suitcase through the rush of people eager to catch their trains. He looks quite different out here, away from the tea table - more vulnerable. His suit jacket stretches tightly across his chest and the trousers are shiny at the knees.

I ask him if he is travelling far and he tells me that he is going to visit his sister in Wimbledon. He has dropped his sophisticated line of chat and seems a little sad.

'Well, goodbye,' he says, putting down his case to shake my hand. 'An interesting event. Colourful at any rate.'

I laugh, agree and we part company.

At the escalator he turns, searches for me, catches my eye and waves.

I wave back then following the signs to Baker Street, catch the Metropolitan train home.

THE CHRISTMAS FARE

Cynthia Gormley-Smythe's meringues were her pride and joy. Neither too chewy nor too crunchy, they fitted the bill to perfection: white clouds of mixed sugar and eggs. Cooked to a tee and arranged on large decorative plates, they were manna from heaven.

No-one could compete with Cynthia. No-one dared.

Dorothy Honey, the vicar's wife, was in charge of the cakes for the Christmas fare. Handed in to the vicarage the day before, they were placed on the dining room table waiting to be priced.

Mrs Smith, the organist's wife, pronounced her sandwich sponge to be every bit as good as Mrs Jones's chocolate sponge, and would Mrs Jones mind telling her how many eggs went into the mixture. Three small? Oh dear me! Hers had four large. That merited a higher price than Mrs Jones's cake, surely.

Dorothy Honey and members of The Mother's Union spent the evening removing sticky labels, replacing sticky labels and tearing up sticky labels. All in the name of keeping the peace.

The cakes varied in size and variety. Cup cakes went down well with the younger shoppers who would eat them on the hoof. The richer fruit cakes went down well with the older parishioners who were no longer up to making their own Christmas cakes. But Cynthia Gormley-Smythe's meringues were the highlight. They were placed at the front of the trestle table for all to see, admire and buy.

She would bring them straight to the village hall having priced them herself. No-one raised an eyebrow or questioned this. That she was deemed exempt from surrendering her fare to the dining room table was not an issue. You did not question Cynthia. She was above criticism. Local gossip seemed to go right over her gracious plait-bound head. Discussion groups and musical evenings were more her line.

The Fare was opened by Lady Privott, a local celebrity and judge of the horticultural shows held every October. The hall was full, the stalls glittered with Christmas sparkle and the cake stall groaned with goodies.

When Lady Privott had finished her speech on the importance of using litter bins ... Was she at the right venue? ... the event was declared open and off she sailed to inspect the different stalls; the church wardens and the vicar meekly following in her wake.

On reaching the cakes, her eyes at once fixed on the meringues.

'Who made these?' she demanded.

'A member of our congregation,' said Dorothy Honey, handing out change to a woman buying a batch of scones.

'But which member of the congregation?' came the insistent reply.

'Why, Cynthia Gormley-Smythe,' said one of the helpers.

Lady Privott flung out her arm - a grand gesture intended to encompass all the produce, and in so doing socked a young lad across the face. He fell backwards causing someone to push her forward thus landing her face down in the meringues. Cream seeped from their seams and onto her face. The snowy white edifices crumpled and collapsed dropping like depressed clouds onto the floor.

Horror! Oh Horror!

Eyes fixed first on Lady Privott's freshly bearded face and then on Cynthia Gormley-Smythe seen buying a potted geranium from the stall next door.

'My meringues!' she hissed, dropping the pot and was beside Lady Privott in an instant. 'Did you drop those?'

'I was pushed,' cried Lady Privott looking about her for the culprit who had vanished. While unnerved and feeling foolish, her sugared jaw remained firm. 'Delicious, I'm sure. But rather too large for the plate, wouldn't you agree?'

'The plate was plenty large enough,' exclaimed Cynthia Gormley-Smythe.

'Then perhaps your meringues could have been smaller?'

'Smaller? You think? Oh, please do feel free to speak your mind.'

'Very well.' Lady Privott drew herself up to her full height. 'In my humble opinion, their size makes them appear a shade vulgar.'

'Vulgar!' cried Cynthia Gormley-Smythe, her face growing purple with rage.

'Forgive my saying so,' Lady Privott was on a roll, 'but your meringues have crowded out the other cakes, cakes that contain more substance. What sustenance is there in a meringue? All sugar. Give me a good old fashioned fruit cake, or a light sponge for those committee tea breaks.'

She pointed at Mrs Smith's Victoria sandwich for which she paid with shaky fingers before continuing on her way; so proving she had more metal than Cynthia Gormley-Smythe who was being shown to a chair and handed a glass of water.

That her meringues were large, was indisputable. But vulgar? A nagging doubt began to worm its way into Cynthia Gormley-Smythe's mind, nibbling at her confidence, self-esteem and very soul. Why had she been tempted to make them so large? The recipe had specified teaspoonfuls not desert spoonfuls of mixture to be placed on non-stick baking trays. Why then had she not followed the recipe to the letter? Was she, like some of the other women cake makers, competitive? And worse, was she seeking attention? Surely not. Surely she was above such things. Or was she? Blast Lady Privott! She had thrown her off course, forced her to look inside herself; something she rarely had the time or inclination to do.

Sitting there, watching the crowds slowly disperse, she admitted to herself that inner reflections made her feel uncomfortable. They required honesty, self effacement. And she was not sure that she possessed either. She would pray about it, she decided. Yes, she would lay some time aside for prayer. With sincere, true humility, she would hand her problem over to God.

Humility was not an issue. In fact it was something she and her late husband had cultivated down to a fine art. Lent, for instance was the perfect time to demonstrate one's meekness. And then there was the church brass. Did she not polish that with her own hands instead of sending her daily to do the job? And how many times had she taken the church collection, visited the sick, collected filthy rummage? But nonetheless she would, indeed she should seek spiritual guidance. And if the worst came to the worst there was always compromise, a word she had never liked using but still - let it never be said that she was unreasonable. Perhaps next year her meringues could be a shade smaller and less white. A touch of vanilla would deal with that. Perhaps also, she could sell them singly and without cream sandwiching the two halves and contributing to their size. Alternatively, she could try making something else: a walnut sponge perhaps?

But as she sat sipping her water and racking her brains for ideas, her heart sank deeper and deeper. Images of her large, voluptuous meringues kept flashing before her eyes. She looked wearily at the cake stall. All gone. Only fragments of her distressed offerings remained scattered over the table cloth, over the side and onto the floor.

Slowly she rose to her feet. No-one stopped her, or spoke to her as she made for the exit. It was almost as though now her meringues had been shattered, she was of no consequence.

Perhaps, she thought as she hurried to the car park, she should hurry along the prayer; offer up her supplication in the car on her way home. It would certainly save time and she had a committee meeting to attend at eight.

Sniffing back the tears she wondered if God understood the more secular aspects of human life; those culinary efforts that could go so horribly wrong resulting in dire consequences. What, oh what had she done to deserve such a humiliating experience at the hands of Lady Privott, whose white grape hyacinths were rumoured to be among the finest in the country.

Reaching some traffic lights, she tried to construct a suitable prayer without the word meringue in it; it seemed rather frivolous and foolish. But the more she tried, the harder it became. No words, no phrases seemed to sum up her predicament ... her feelings of anger, humiliation; of hurt pride and failure.

The lights turned orange. Cynthia Gormley-Smythe let out the clutch and revved up the engine. It was then she noticed in the distance a woman standing by the side of her car on the grass verge. She looked, she peered, she gasped. Surely not. It couldn't be. But yes, it was. It definitely was: Lady Privott, all hot and bothered frantically thumbing a lift. Her offside wheel looked very flat indeed.

The lights turned green. Cynthia Gormley-Smythe shot ahead. But try as she may, she could not rid herself of the picture of Lady Privott stranded by the roadside. She wondered why she was not gloating, or, had her hands been free, rubbing them with glee at seeing her rival so dislodged and fretful. Instead, to her utmost surprise, she felt sorry for the woman. How ghastly to be stuck with a puncture in the middle of the country. Not many people passed that way, and in any case, you were never quite sure these days who could be trusted.

Thoughts of a kindly nature were now nudging her to take action. With beating heart, she made her decision. She would turn round, drive back and go to Lady Privott's assistance.

As she reversed, she smiled ruefully. God answered prayers in so many unexpected ways. Cynthia Gormley-Smythe's meringues may be large, they may even be vulgar but she certainly knew how to mend a puncture.

THE PICNIC

'Why are you sitting on the hamper?' he asks.

'Just resting,' I say.

'You'll dent it! Move yourself. I want to check.'

'No need. Everything's there.'

Please God the lid doesn't give way.

'Roger and Jemima coming?'

'You know they are.'

He scans the room as though checking for missiles.

'Flowers!'

I jump. 'Flowers?'

'You haven't picked any.'

'Their garden's awash with flowers. Why add to them?'

He sighs. Looks at his problem wife sitting, buttocks clenched on his beloved food hamper.

'Don't you want to go?'

'Not really, no.'

'Time of the month is it?'

'No.'

'We should go: Our fifth time. Remember?'

Oh, I remember. Who would not remember The Rawlings' Picnics?

'Dinner alfresco, darlings: Bring the inside out.' Prudence's invitations: insistent little commands issued annually from tight, suburban lips. 'Guests bring their own tables and chairs, food and wine. We provide the grounds. Our garden's a riot of colour late September. We want to share it with our friends. You'll come of course.'

Of course. When The Rawlings summon, you obey. So over these past few years I've planned our menu with artillery-like precision. My husband, a retired major, expects an efficient wife. And I do try.

So, into the food hamper go wild salmon, pheasants, meringues, the best cheeses, pates, hand-made chocolates. There's not, has never been the merest whiff of an egg sandwich. Certainly not!

Aubrey, a stickler for good form, insists we include the silver plated cutlery, china plates, white linen napkins, cloth and candles. The amount we take, a caravan of camels would come in handy. We even pick flowers to decorate our table, for God's Sake: Which brings me to the garden furniture. Nothing gives Aubrey greater pleasure than shopping for picnic tables, chairs, umbrellas and every conceivable outside appliance. Yes, everything is planned down to the last coffee spoon.

'Come on Charlotte! Stop playing silly buggers. What's the main course? I need to pack the wine.' He researches that too. What wine to drink with what.

'It's red meat, Aubrey,' is all I say.

'What red meat? Let me see.'

My heart races. 'No.'

'Why not?'

'It's a surprise. If I get up from here, you'll open the basket to do your damn checking. You know what you're like. And this time, just for once, I don't want you to. Okay?'

His eyes narrow. 'Not like you, Charlotte - surprises. All right, I'll take a couple of bottles of the *Beaujolais Fleurie*. Hope you've packed some of that game pie. Oh, and did you clean the cutlery? Last year the forks had a slightly tarnished look to them, I thought.'

'Yes, yes.'

'Good. I'll go and get the chairs from the garage. Then we must move.'

Slam! he's gone. I cringe. Stare at my small, sandaled feet. Sam said I had pretty feet, fairy feet. I wiggle my toes and wonder if he's arrived yet.

'Do we want these old picture frames of yours?'

Aubrey likes yelling through walls. He won't come and ask me anything, just shouts through six inches of brick.

'I'm chucking this lot out next week, the whole damn lot. Do you hear?'

Crash!

'Bugger!'

Bang! He's back.

'They're not there Charlotte!'

I rise slowly to my feet. Walk over to the sink and speak her name.

'Jemima.'

'Jemima?' He's on the alert now.

'She's got them.' And my legs shake like jelly, like they did when I had my breakdown ten years back.

'Got our chairs?' There is panic in his voice.

'Yes.'

He stares dumb-founded. 'What in heaven's name is Jemima doing with our chairs?'

I fill my little watering can and drench the geraniums blooming nicely on the window sill.

'Last year, after the picnic,' I say, 'you went to look at the Rawlings' new air-conditioned kitchen. Jemima and I were packing things away …'

He taps his foot.

'Don't do that, Aubrey.'

'Get on with it, then.'

'She said how much she liked them.'

'Well, yes. I paid good money for those chairs. *Harrod*'s sale: summer '06.'

'Quite.'

'So?'

'She wanted them.'

'Is that it?'

'Yes.'

'She wanted them?'

'Yes.'

'So you gave them to her? Just like that?'

'Not gave them Aubrey, lent. She said that her picnic chairs were not fit to sit on; asked if we'd mind lending ours. So I agreed. After all, we only use them at The Rawlings'. Roger and Jemima go to more picnics than we do.'

Two red petals fall onto the draining board: two drops of blood. I turn. Face him. He can't argue, you see, not about Jemima: She with the Titian hair, the thirty-eight inch bust and the heart murmur.

'I wish you'd asked me, Charlotte. You should always ask.'

'I'm sorry, Aubrey.'

'They're bringing them, I hope?'

'Oh, yes.'

Thump, thump my heart.

'You really should have told me. Can't understand you, Charlotte. Letting me search in the garage like an idiot. Thought it was strange. Remember - stacking 'em away last year. Never forget a thing like that. What's wrong with you?'

There's no answer to that. There is a lot wrong with me.

The hamper stands large and square in the middle of the floor.

Pang! My guilt clock. Pang! Pang!

I shouldn't have done this: Committed this act. I'm not the type. But even now it may not be too late. If I can get him out of here, there may still be time.

His eyes do another scan.

'Doors, windows locked? Answer machine on? Charged the mobile, have you?'

'Look, Aubrey, why don't you go and pick those flowers?'

'Not now! Should have thought of that before. There's the traffic. Must go. Come on!'

It is too late! If only my pulse would slow down. Perhaps I'll have a heart attack and die on the way. Solve everything. Calm! Must stay calm! Breathe slowly, steadily. Good.

Aubrey stares at the hamper. Please God, don't let him open it. Not yet.

'Help me lift this into the car, Charlotte.'

I reach for the handle. My hands shake.

'Lift!'

We stagger outside. God! It's heavy. The boot is open ready. The hamper slides home with the ease of a coffin on runners. He stands back; admires his handy-work. Eyes glitter with pleasure.

'There!' He rubs his hands. 'A place for everything and everything in its place.'

Oh yes, think I, climbing into the front seat: everything in its place. My hand reaches behind, feels for the rear foot well. It is still there. Nothing has been touched.

Forty minutes later and here we are; and there are Rupert and Prudence Rawlings standing at the gate telling everyone where to go. Give the two of them uniforms and they'd make perfect traffic wardens.

People trail across the lawn, carrying their chattels like refugees. There must be at least eighty guests. Some have already de-camped: want to keep their regular spots, I suppose.

There's Gwen and Owen Pugh sitting under the *Wisteria floribunda*. Careful Owen. Don't want to do yourself a mischief blowing up that plastic ice bucket.

And Bernard and Maisie Hughes play it safe on the patio, just like last year and the year before. Bernard's prostate, you know. 'We're close to the loo here,' says Maisie, giving her hands a brisk wipe on a paper towelette.

Oh God! Not The Pelham-Browns and that ghastly Jack Russell of theirs. What's he called? Raffles, that's it. She's just let him off the lead.

I expect he'll wee over everything. Ghastly animal! Can't think why The Rawlings allow dogs. Oh, but of course! They're best, best friends, darling!

Ah! Aubrey has just spotted Jemima and Roger sitting on striped deckchairs. Over we go to the rockery.

I stare at Jemima, slim and frail and draped in cream silk.

Jemima stares at Aubrey.

And Aubrey stares at the deckchairs.

Roger delves into his hold-all. 'Seen my acrylic corkscrew, Jemmy? Hi, you two! Brought a bottle opener, I hope. What are you staring at, Aubrey?'

'Where did you get those chairs, Roger?' Iron control.

'Prudence lent us the last two. Jemmy's a bit off colour today. And you were a bit late turning up; thought you might not be coming.'

Jemima smiles: the smile is for Aubrey. It says he could have her now if the rest of us weren't there.

'But our picnic chairs,' splutters Aubrey, ignoring her. 'Where are our picnic chairs?' This is the nearest I've seen him to tears, since the day his mother gave his teddy bear to *Oxfam*.

Roger shrugs. 'Thought *you* were bringing them.'

'No! You were.' He'll stamp his foot in a minute. 'Charlotte lent them to Jemima last year. Don't say you haven't brought them?'

Jemima lifts exquisite shoulders. 'Not me, darling.'

Roger reaches for his zip-up wine cooler.

'No need to get excited, Aubrey. How could we bring them if we haven't got them? Pass that bottle of wine, will you, Jemmy.'

Aubrey grips my arm and steers me roughly to one side. He opens his mouth to speak and swallows some of Stephanie Sullivan's mosquito repellent.

'The chairs,' he chokes. 'Where are they?'

'You're hurting my arm, Aubrey.'

'You'll both join us later, for coffee?' calls Melanie Pelham-Brown scooping *Pedigree Chum* into a dog bowl.

'We'd love to,' I call back: Must keep my voice steady.

'What are you playing at Charlotte?' Aubrey through clenched teeth.

'Jemima's got our chairs, I told you.'

'She says that she hasn't.'

'Look, we can sit on a rug,' I offer by way of recompense.

'A rug?' His jaw drops. With a bit of luck he'll swallow more repellent. 'We can't sit on a rug!'

'Why not?'

'For a start, we didn't pack a rug.'

'I did.'

His little eyes bulge.

'You?'

'Yes.'

'I didn't see you pack a rug.'

'It's on the floor by the back seat - the rear foot well. I'll go and get it.'

'You won't!' A thin spray of saliva hits my eye. Venom! 'Look around you, Charlotte. Can you see anyone here sitting on rugs?'

'No, but …'

'No-one sits on rugs - not here - not at The Rawlings'.'

'That doesn't mean to say that we can't.' I can be stubborn at times.

'Don't be ridiculous.'

'But why can't we?'

'Because everyone here sits on chairs around tables. It's the way it's done.'

There's an expensive rustle from behind. Rupert and Prudence Rawlings are on their way to the top table. They climb their rose-infested bank, smile and wave.

Jemima yawns, raises her glass and winks at Aubrey.

'All right, you two?' Prudence calls, helping herself to a French stick.

'We're fine, Prue. Just fine,' calls back Aubrey, flashing recently veneered teeth. But his face glowers red in the light of twenty flares edging the lawn.

The band plays, *Blue Moon*.

'What are you doing?' trills Jemima, waving her wine glass at us. 'Come and have drinkies. Roger's found the bottle opener.'

Another flash of those teeth. 'Be with you in a sec. Must put up our table first. You carry on.'

I glance at our picnic table propped against a young pear tree. (Prudence has sprayed the fruit gold). The table looks funny minus its matching chairs: kind of lonely.

Last year Aubrey and Jemima had sat on two of them - sat close, laughing and joking, the way lovers do. Later they disappeared for a whole hour - didn't say where they were going, or how long they'd be. Just left.

Roger acted as though he didn't care: whistled between his teeth and drank a lot. He didn't talk much and in the end I couldn't stand his infernal whistling and those empty chairs, so I wandered up the garden, past laughing couples drinking coffees and brandy, to where the band was playing an old Shirley Bassey number, *Hands Across The Sea*.

The evening was warm. I took off my sandals and danced. The grass spiked my feet. The heady effects of the wine coupled with the music soothed me. I felt safe: cocooned amidst the couples swaying cheek to cheek.

That was when I saw Sam. He was playing the base guitar, his long, blonde hair tied back in a ponytail, the way they did it in the eighties. He caught me staring. I blushed and smiled. He smiled back. I felt silly now dancing on my own in the moonlight. But I carried on anyway: shuffling my feet, feeling the grass, smelling the night.

After the number finished there was an interval and Sam came over and introduced himself. He was nice. His eyes were a quiet grey and he smiled a lot. That was the evening he told me I had pretty feet. For the first time in years I felt young, attractive and wanted. We exchanged telephone numbers.

The next day Aubrey was away playing in a golf tournament. I felt excited, on a high, kept listening for the 'phone to ring.

I decided to clean out the garage. Hard, physical work might take my mind off the previous night - off Aubrey, Jemima, Sam.

Sam! At least sixteen years younger than I was. Ridiculous to think he might ring. What would he want with a woman of my age?

The garage was full of junk: half-used pots of household paint, a pair of Aubrey's old skis, receipts and bills going back years. There were old suitcases, books, papers. Under a moth-eaten blanket was a *Black Magic* chocolate box. I opened it. Inside were ten letters addressed to Aubrey. I shouldn't have opened them, but I did. They were love letters written years back from some poor woman who had been duped by him. Their affair hadn't lasted long, but then his affairs rarely did. I read one or two: sentimental, sad little notes. That he had not bothered to destroy them or at least lock them away seemed to me the worst insult of all.

Anger is a potent fuel and I worked feverishly. By mid-afternoon most of the rubbish had been packed into plastic bags. My old gilt picture frames could stay: they might be worth something. All that remained to be cleared were some old magazines stacked high on a shelf next to the electric meter. But I hadn't the energy to deal with those: later perhaps. Yes, I would deal with them another time.

It was then that my eyes rested on the picnic chairs. Aubrey had stacked them the previous night in readiness for next year. How I loathed those stainless steel frames and fat, red plush seats. A plan began to form in my head. If I re-arranged one or two bags of rubbish, they would probably just fit into the boot of my car.

Half an hour later I set off for the local tip; speeding through the back streets my heart racing at what I was about to do.

First to go over the side was the rubbish: one, two, three, four large sacks.

I paused for breath. This was my moment! The moment I'd been waiting for. I lifted the chairs out of the boot and arranged them in a row by the railings.

'Someone would be glad of those,' I overheard a woman say, but my body was pumped too full of adrenaline to care.

Fantasy went into overdrive. I was the executioner. The prisoners: Jemima and Aubrey.

Jemima was first. I lifted her high into the air, paused then slowly tantalizingly dropped her over the side. She fell with characteristic grace into an empty cement bag.

Aubrey! I placed the box of love letters onto his lap and lifted him over the side. His short legs dangled perilously. I granted him one final request which was pretty generous of me, I thought. Not surprisingly, he chose to make a speech. It took the form of a reproof: how I'd fallen short of my wifely duties, my untidiness, lack of intellect, lack of dress sense, lack of glamour ...

Enough! Your time is up!

I threw him. Hard. He dropped straight into the jaws of a mechanical shovel.

I left the two remaining chairs by the side. Someone could have those. I climbed into my car, slammed shut the door and drove off.

'Charlotte, stop dreaming. You can go and open the hamper now.' Aubrey bangs home the final bolt then shakes the table hard. 'Seems firm enough.'

'No.' I splutter. 'You must open the hamper. Remember? It's your surprise.'

Please God, don't let him make me do it!

'Get sorted, for Pete's sake,' calls Roger, filling his wineglass to the brim. 'We're starting our food, okay? Don't mind if we don't wait, do you? Only we're famished.'

'All done,' says Aubrey, carrying the table over to the others.

'Shouldn't we find something to sit on?' I ask. Now the moment has come and I can hardly bare it.

Aubrey glowers. 'Thanks to your cock up, Charlotte, we'll have to eat standing.'

Roger starts to get up. 'Look, have my deckchair.'

'No, thank you, Roger. Charlotte and I will stand.'

Roger shrugs. 'Please yourselves.'

Aubrey's lower lip quivers as he grabs the hamper, tears at the leather straps, jerks open the lid. 'So what's this ruddy surprise then?' But the words die on his lips as he looks inside. Sees, stares, motionless. Slowly, very slowly he lowers the lid. Hooded eyes meet mine.

I am screaming inside. No, no, I didn't do it. It wasn't me. This is the worst nightmare of my life.

'What's wrong, Aubrey?' asks Roger. 'Found a snake in there, or something?'

I turn away; search familiar faces. The Smythe-Jones! They'll do; over by the gazebo, filling their mucid mouths with avocado pears. I join them. Suddenly crave to be part of their pedestrian lives.

A minute later, Jemima's voice: strident, insistent asking Aubrey to dance. I turn. Dare to look. He's sitting on the hamper. Guarding it. Jemima tries to pull him to his feet. 'You don't mind if I borrow your husband do you, Charlotte?' she calls.

'Feel free.'

Oh, she feels that all right.

Jemima starts tickling his ribs. He laughs. Hysterical, he begs her to stop, curls into a ball. He's very susceptible to tickling, is my husband. There was a time, early on in our marriage when he liked me to tickle him. I watch and my stomach turns.

I glance over at Roger. His face is puce, diffused with rage. I've never seen him angry before. Slowly, deliberately, he heaves his pot bellied six-foot frame out of the deckchair, staggers across to Aubrey and looms over him.

'Lay off her!'

The Smythe-Jones laugh, embarrassed. They don't want any trouble.

I make my excuses and wander back.

Aubrey ignores me: his chin set in defiance.

'Quieten down, Rog, old thing.'

'Think I don't know, Aubrey?' Roger sneers.

'You're drunk!'

'Not as drunk as I'd like to be.'

'Cool it, will you?'

'You're screwing my wife. You bastard!'

Stephanie Sullivan drops a cocktail sausage into her wineglass.

'Don't be bloody ridiculous, Roger,' squeals Jemima.

'You stay out of this,' he snarls giving her a shove as he leans his weight against the hamper and pushes hard. 'Lay off my wife, you understand?'

'Steady!' Aubrey hangs on. 'No need to get rough!'

But Roger keeps pushing with Jemima screeching in the background. Back and forth, faster and faster and all the while his eyes fix menacingly on Aubrey's face.

People gather round. What's going on? Is this a game? Have The Rawlings laid on entertainment?

And now Roger brings his full weight to bear. One final shove. The hamper overturns. Aubrey is on his knees.

Everyone cheers. They clap, stamp and call for more.

Jemima runs to Aubrey's side.

'Leave him!' Roger booms.

She pulls back, startled by his tone.

Aubrey staggers to his feet, straightens his tie, tucks his shirt into his trousers and catches sight of The Pughes and The Hughes standing giggling in a little group.

I've never seen Aubrey look so furious. He's so incensed he must have forgotten about the hamper lying on its side, lid half open. Instead he strides across to our ice cooler, ignores me standing there and grabs a bottle of whiskey.

Raffles barks hysterically, jumps out of Melanie's arms, straight onto Stephanie Sullivan's lap. She shrieks and drops a plate of salad. A half-eaten chicken leg flies into the air and lands just inside the upturned hamper. Raffles lifts his head, leaps off Stephanie and makes a dive for it.

'He'll choke!' screams Melanie and rushing forward bends and scoops the dog into her arms. He bares his teeth and growls, as she prises the bone from his jaws. It drops inside the hamper. She stoops to retrieve it. Stops and stares.

'Good God!'

She rushes over to Stephanie and whispers in her ear. Stephanie's eyes widen. They stare first at the hamper then at Aubrey looking morose over by the ice cooler.

Soon The Pughs, The Hughes and The Smythe-Jones saunter over to the hamper with casual intent. They look, whisper and glance furtively at Aubrey. He slopes, whiskey bottle in hand, towards a large Grecian urn behind which he will doubtless drown his sorrows.

Jemima stays close to Roger - the safer option - while he packs their belongings into the hold all. She chooses not to look. Poor Jemima! She'll thank me in years to come.

And Rupert and Prudence? Well, they've descended from their grassy bank, expressed displeasure and issued a new proclamation that in future all picnic invitations will be issued to close friends only.

That's me out then.

I look at my watch. It is time to go.

A brief nod from Maisie Pelham-Brown and Raffles growls and nips my ankles. The Pughes throw me a look of pity. How could I live with such a man? The Smythe-Jones ask if they can help, which is kind. I tell them, no. That I am used to my husband and his unorthodox ways.

The Sullivans have already left, leaving in their wake a trail of lettuce leaves: a small reminder of the night's foray. The rest of the guests are dispersing. 'Good night.' 'Good night.'

The lawn is pretty tidy all things considered: that says something for the Rawlings' friends, close or otherwise. Only a single white, table napkin flaps haphazardly in the breeze.

My heart lightens with each new step.

Close now.

At first he does not see me. I stop. Wait - every nerve taut.

'Hello Sam.'

He turns: those eyes that tell me I am special meet mine. And I glow. Oh, how I glow!

'There's been a bit of bother here to-night, did you hear?' he asks, placing his jacket around my shoulders. I stiffen: don't want re-plays, not just now, not from him. I shake my head and watch him place his guitar lovingly into its case and zip it up.

'Yeah,' he says. 'Apparently someone told our drummer that a guest, some major or other, brought in a load of porn mags. He'd packed them in a picnic hamper. There was no food in it just magazines: stacks of them. Quite old some of them too. Some folk are really weird, aren't they?' He raises his eyes - smiles that special smile that tells me I am loved for sure. 'There was a bit of a fight as well. You must have heard!'

I shake my head. 'I went for a stroll.'

Sam nods. He believes me. I shouldn't lie - not to Sam.

He says goodbye to the lads. Tells them he'll see them at next week's gig.

And then, 'Ready?'

'Ready.'

'Have you brought a suitcase?' he asks, as we hurry down the drive.

'Of course.' I squeeze his hand and feel for the car keys in my pocket. 'It's under the rug in the car.'

TIN WEDDING

It all started the evening I opened that tin of potatoes.

Robert came into the kitchen saying he wanted to talk to me. Robert hardly ever came into the kitchen. In the old days kitchens used to be women's domains. It had certainly been mine for the last ten years, or so I thought.

'Can't it wait 'til after dinner?' I had my back to him.

'No Ann, it can't.' His voice sounded insistent and edgy.

'What is it then?'

He paused, shuffled from one foot to the other, coughed and shuffled some more.

'Well, spit it out Robert.'

'Very well. I'm having an affair Ann. With Hilary.'

And that was when the opener jammed and I sprained my wrist.

'Hilary?' I screeched, swinging round to face him. 'Hilary! Your secretary?'

He nodded, his face grave and pink.

'Look Ann. I'm terribly sorry. I understand how you must feel. It must be an awful shock. And if you want me to leave now, I'll pack a bag and ...' He broke off, saw me nursing my hand. 'Are you all right love?'

'Do I look all right?' I yelled, the pain kicking in. 'I've just sprained my wrist on this bloody tin of potatoes.'

Well, you could have cut the silence with a knife.

'You know I never eat tinned potatoes, Ann.' His voice sepulchral and low.

I brandished the tin opener warrior-like in front of his face.

'Let me tell you,' I screeched harridan style, 'You've had tinned potatoes many times. And not just potatoes either: tinned rice, tinned prunes, tinned stew, tinned tomatoes. You name it, you've had it. Tinned.'

'Here?' he breathed, his face ashen. 'Here, in this house?'

I swear all thoughts of Hilary swept from his mind as I watched him grapple with this revelation. Robert's fastidious. Very. He likes things smooth running; loves his home comforts - including meals cooked by his loving attentive wife. And I am - was a good cook. Too good. It doesn't pay to be too good on the domestic front, if you want a life to call your own.

Soon after we got married I took up painting as a hobby. Hobbies can be dangerous too, if you become addicted to them which is exactly what I did. Not at first. At first, for the first six months or so, I cooked properly - nothing instant, nothing frozen but all home baked, home cooked food, from the plain Victoria sponge, the scrubbed potatoes, the rice puddings and egg custards to the plucking of the odd pheasant and jugging hares. No cutting corners. Absolutely not. It was only later when I became hopelessly hooked on oil painting that things began to change. I just loved it and would have painted all day if I had had my way. Glossy, rich seductive oils applied to large or small canvases. And as time has gone by my pictures have begun to sell and for the first time in ten years of married life, I'm making some money. Wonderful! The trouble is, that art and the love of it thereof has left me little or no time to rustle up those gastronomic delights that Robert had become so accustomed to. It's a while since I cooked goujons of sole with shrimp sauce, he loves sauces, and heaven knows when I last made a batch of apple jelly jam - a sweet tooth has Robert.

So to get round this rather sensitive predicament, to save time and energy, I began, slowly at first, to introduce the odd tin or two. I became what you might call crafty, but which I would call creative. Well, you know, one just has to get by the best way one can.

But back to the present. Now steaming with undiluted rage and pain I demanded to know how long he'd been having this affair.

'One year,' he announced. Then wanted to know how long I had been using cans.

'Three,' I said, stretching it a bit.

'And all that time I thought ...'

'You thought I'd been slogging over a hot stove. Well, wrong!'

'Before we married, Ann, you promised we'd never eat out of tins.'

'Is that the only reason you tied the knot - for my culinary skills?'

Robert dropped stone-like onto the nearest chair:

'I'd no idea you cooked instant food on the cheap. Don't I give you enough house-keeping? Where do you keep them all?'

'I hoard them. Like an alcoholic, I stack them away in secret places so you won't find them.'

His recently shaped eyebrows shot up in amazement.

Determined to press on, I reminded him of my time-consuming passion adding how most people, including Delia Smith probably succumbed to tinned food from time to time. Modern life was hectic and gone were the days when women were tied to the sink or the stove.

'The trouble with you, Robert, is that you're so egotistical, so opinionated, you really believe you can tell margarine from butter. But the truth is, you can't. And I've proved it.'

For the first time in our married life, Robert was speechless. His shoulders stooped and he looked suddenly old. I felt a pang of guilt. Compared with me, Hilary now took on saint-like qualities. Doubtless she would never serve up heavily disguised - I usually added clever little touches to the soups and fruits to pass muster - tins of instant food. And yet here I was, all set to celebrate my tenth wedding anniversary, not having chalked up a single snog with another man, let alone an affair, feeling as guilty as Hell.

Robert took a bottle of Chardonnay from the fridge.

'We'll have this, shall we - with the fish?' He nodded in the direction of two salmon fillets, lying pink and sleek next to the microwave. 'I see the fish is fresh, at least.'

As we ate in silence I wondered what to give him for pudding. I'd been planning on opening a tin of mandarin oranges. If you drain them and shake a little sweetened flour over the segments, they really do pass for the real thing and taste splendid with cognac poured over them.

But there was no pudding.

Instead, Robert rose from the table - slammed the kitchen door and went upstairs.

I crept into the hall and listened. I heard the shower go, the whine of his battery toothbrush, the rumble of the electric razor and the pull of the lavatory chain. Finally Robert emerged, his fluffy white towel tied around a thickening middle. He pulled down the loft ladder and disappeared into its gaping hole.

I waited - my heart pounding.

There were a series of thumps as Robert, gleaming water drops, lugged my worst fear down the ladder onto the landing.

'So this is where you hide them Ann! In my *Harrod's* suitcase!'

He threw open the lid, seized a can of mixed beans in one hand, and a ninety-nine per cent fat free tin of stewing-steak in the other and shook them like castanets. I'd never seen him so angry.

'How dare you assault my taste buds!' he yelled, flinging tins hither and thither.

They rolled, they bounced. They bashed the banisters, dented the doors and scratched the walls. Robert then snatched up the emptied case, marched into our bedroom and slammed the door.

Oh! I longed for him to hurry, to go: craved a silence filled only by the sound of soft brushes against canvas.

My latest client, with the palest blue eyes, likes my work: thinks it innovative and brave. There's talk of an exhibition. He thinks I'm promising, you see.

A warm glow began to creep over me and when Robert finally re-emerged in stockinged feet, wearing his red jersey and designer jeans, I felt quite calm and unruffled.

'Hilary will make you a better wife,' I said dreamily.

'To hell with Hilary!' he stormed, and took his first step of descent.

The landing was dark, the carpeted stairs steep and straight. He didn't see the tins of tomatoes, two for the price of one, lurking two steps down. His right foot hit them, rolled over them. He slipped and with a startled cry tumbled to the bottom, where he lay groaning and cursing at my feet.

I walked to the telephone, and dialled Hilary's number.

'It's Ann, Robert's wife,' I said. 'You can come and collect him now. He's all yours.'

WHERE THE BEE SUCKS

The king was in his counting house counting out his money, the queen was in the parlour eating bread and ...

'Where's my honey!' she screamed.

The king sighed, 'Not again!'

He left off counting and wearily made his way to his bed chamber. So much gold, so many riches and such a frightful wife.

He took two wax ear-plugs from his bedside drawer, stuck them deep into his ears and lay down. Leaning across the bed he opened a large box of chocolates, a gift from the king of Spain. His eyes ran over the selection of goodies. Ah! A mint creme. He picked it, bit it, savoured the sharp sweet taste. There was nothing like sugar to calm the nerves. He was about to choose another, when the door flung open and there the queen stood, her face black with rage.

'When will you sort out your bees Bertram? It's mid-summer and there should be a large supply of honey. I have nothing to put on my bread. And what are you doing lying down when you should be standing up and counting our money. We need every coin we can get. There is a recession if you hadn't noticed.'

She eyed the chocolates, her face softened and her hands reached out. Licking her lips, she dipped her fat ringed fingers into the box, and drew out a strawberry creme.

'The trouble with you, Bertha dear,' said the king watching her keenly, 'is that you don't have sufficient to do.'

'True,' she confessed licking her sticky plump lips.

Well, that's a start, thought the king sitting up and placing an arm around her ample waist.

'Would you like to take charge of the bees? Become one of the bee keepers perhaps? That would be a pleasant diversion. And I'm sure they could do with some extra help.'

'You really think I could?' Chocolate dribbled down her chin as she reached for another.

The king slapped her hand. 'Not that one, dearest. You know full well that the nutty whirls are mine.'

'So, I'll eat the one next to it.'

This time his hand came down harder.

'That's a toffee caramel,' he snarled. 'My second favourite. Buy your own chocolates, Bertha. It's not as though I leave you short of cash.'

She was foraging amongst the wrappings. 'Where are the marzipans? There should be two on each layer.'

The king snatched the red plush box and peered inside. 'Looks like they've gone. I must have eaten them.'

'But marzipans are *my* favourites. The King of Spain gave this box to both of us and what do you do? Hog the lot.'

'Now, Bertha. Don't take on. Remember your blood pressure. Calm down and concentrate on your new, exciting venture with the bees.'

'Did you or did you not take the marzipans from this box?'

'Possibly, yes. By mistake though. It was not deliberate.'

'How could you! My own husband denying me the one pleasure I love above all else?'

'Oh come now,' said the King, removing his ear-plugs, 'Don't you think that you're being a little over dramatic. They're only chocolates after all.'

'That's not the point,' snapped the queen. 'It's a matter of principle.'

'Very well,' sighed the king. 'Let's go through the rules again: You take the lemon delights, the strawberry cremes, the orange cremes and the marzipan, and leave the nuttys and the nougats and the peppermint cremes for me. Now, I couldn't be fairer than that, could I?'

'When you put it like that, I suppose not,' sulked the queen, adjusting her crown. 'But haven't you forgotten two other important chocolates.'

'Have I?'

'You forgot to mention the caramels and the Turkish Delights.'

He walked over to the window and looked out onto the palace gardens.

'Such a beautiful sunny summer's day, I think that I'll give my counting a break and go for a walk.'

'Don't change the subject. Face it, Bertram. You're a cheat. You cheat at Snap, you cheat at snakes and ladders and now this.'

'Snakes and ladders? Never.'

'I saw you go up that snake instead of down.'

'Surely not. When?'

'The other afternoon when you thought I wasn't looking. And now, you deliberately omit mentioning the caramels and the Turkish Delights. You're a cheat. That's what you are.'

He paused: How best could he humour her?

'Very well. I'll tell you what we'll do. We'll share the caramels and the Turkish delights. How about that?'

'You say that. But can I trust you?'

The king was about to answer when the maid entered. He thought how prettily she curtsied and how slim her waist was in comparison to his wife's.

'Excuse me, your majesties. But something awful 'as 'appened.'

'What?' demanded the king.

'The bees 'ave gone.'

'Gone? Gone where?'

'That I cannot say, sir.'

'But that's terrible. I must come at once and see for myself.' And the king ran out of the room leaving the queen alone with the confectionaries.

'No bees, no honey,' she wailed. How shall I comfort myself in the light of such terrible news? She took out a white laced handkerchief and dabbed her eyes. She waddled to the window and watched the king and the maid cross, rather jauntily, she thought, the large lawns bordered by shrubs and beech trees.

What it was to have a king for a husband. Such a burden, especially when his majesty would leave boxes of chocolates all over the place. She peered into the box. There was one left - a coffee creme. She didn't like coffee cremes. She tossed it aside, and lifted the tissue paper that separated the layers. She fed first her eyes and then her mouth with the sumptuous delights that lay beneath: marzipan, nougat, fruit cremes, peppermint cremes, truffles, caramels and Turkish Delights - all waiting, all begging to be consumed. Starting with a truffle, she systematically made her way through all of them ... well, almost all of them.

Dusk had begun to fall, throwing dark shadows across the room, the bed and the contents of the chocolate box. The queen, now compelled to finish what she had begun, squinted at the remaining few. But as it was growing dark, she couldn't see clearly, and she was too full to get up and switch the light on. So, she felt for what was left instead.

Suddenly the queen let out a cry of pain. She screamed and withdrew her hand. A bee hung onto her finger. She tried to brush it off but still it clung. Picking up the box, she smashed it over her hand. The bee fell to the ground dead. But the wound remained.

She sucked, she picked, she ran to the King's counting house and took one of his metal coins and rubbed it hard onto the poorly finger. There was nothing like money to take the sting out of things.

A sudden commotion outside and the king burst in, followed by the maid who was holding her nose and quietly moaning.

'No bees to be seen anywhere,' he said, removing his ermine fringed cloak. 'And poor Maisie's lost her nose.'

'Don't be ridiculous Bertram,' snapped the queen nursing her finger. 'You can't lose your nose. You can follow it, look down it, blow it, but you can't mislay it.'

'It's true, I say. We were inspecting the empty hives when a blackbird, without any warning or provocation, suddenly swooped down and pecked it off. Just like that. Isn't that so, Maisie?'

Maisie nodded and moaned some more.

'I must call the doctor at once. You'll need plastic surgery Maisie, to put it back. I thought we could use your surgeon Bertha. The one who gave you your latest face lift.'

'Please yourself,' snapped the queen. 'I have been stung by one of your horrid bees. Not that you'd care.'

'Really? That reminds me, I was talking to one of the gardeners, Bertha. I asked him what he thought of this sudden migration of bees.'

'Did you hear what I said, Bertram?'

'Yes my love. As *I* was saying, the gardener thinks that we ought to create a more bee friendly environment; more of the cottage garden ... and less of the formal ... to encourage the honey bees, you see. Create more pollinators. That way they won't desert us.'

'One didn't. It landed in the chocolates.'

'I wonder why. Honey bees rarely sting.'

'This one did. But I'll tell you one thing.'

'And what's that Bertha?'

'I won't touch another damned chocolate as long as I live.'

MICHAEL'S TIME OUT

'First name, please?' asks the receptionist, looking up from her desk.

'Michael,' I say, swallowing hard.

She refers to a sheet of paper and performs a neat tick.

'Straight ahead, Michael.'

Straight ahead? How do you go straight ahead when you don't know if you're up, down or sideways on?

She peers at my blank expression and sighs:

'See that castellated cloud over there?' She is pointing to a towering cumulus mass in the distance. And when I nod bleakly: 'That's the one. They're waiting for you there. You had better hurry. They don't like being kept waiting.'

I ask who *they* are. Not an unreasonable question since I haven't the faintest clue where I am, or how I got here. She tells me with a sniff and a dismissive wave of the hand that I will be informed presently. Snooty cow!

There's nothing, nothing about! At all! Well, only clouds. Masses of them: tangled, dappled, domed … I could be in an aeroplane, I feel so high up. And what's under my feet? Feels ever so soft; reminds me of Rita's mum's new carpet.

My stomach! I could be sick. Calm down! Take slow breaths and think, man, think! Right. I left work, that much I *do* remember … was on my way to Liverpool Street Station to catch the 5.25 home to Monkton Priors. I was early, so stopped off in a café for a coffee. There was this young man sat opposite me: I remember him because he had unnaturally blonde hair and piercing blue eyes. We got to chatting, and as we talked, I had the funniest feeling he knew all about me. Strange that. Very strange. He was nice though: different but nice.

Whoops! What's happening to my feet? My feet are on the move … feels like I'm on a travelator … past one cloud then another and another. But hang on! I'm slowing down now … coming closer and closer to a very large cloud, a towering mass of a cloud with what looks like battlements on top of it. This is it! This is the one! A towering white cumulus! Oh, I'm going inside; gliding into the cloud - floating inside it, I am. It's a lovely feeling. Phew! It quite takes your breath away, it really does.

Oh I say! What whiteness! Dazzling! And everything so fluffy! But hang on. Who are those two men sitting over there? Behind that rectangular table? Are they the ones I'm supposed to see? Is this going to be an interview or what?

'Excuse me, sirs. Have I come to the right place?'

They're nodding. Look ever so serious.

'Come closer, Michael,' they say. What deep voices. 'Take a seat.'

Oops! Here we go again! My feet on the move. Could do with a bit of this at home; might get up those stairs of mine a bit quicker.

I'm sat opposite them now, on this plush high-backed chair. It's ever so grand: Upholstered in deep red velvet. It reminds me of one of Rita's finds at those antique fairs she likes to go to. She's made friends with this furniture restorer at the minute. Over the last few weeks, he's been teaching her how to French polish our coffee table. Kind of him, I suppose. Oh heck! She'll be that worried wondering where I am. Punctual to a fault, is my wife. Five days a week for the past twenty years, she's driven me to and from Monkton Priors station so as I can catch my early train to the city. Loyal! What more could a man want?

'Michael!' That's them again.

'Yes?' I say.

'We're pleased you could come,' they chorus.

'I didn't have much option.' Short and to the point, that's me when I'm pushed. Well, things like this don't happen every day. I should hope not!

'We're sorry to inconvenience you, Michael,' they say. 'We don't wish to alarm.' Like heck, they don't. One of them is tapping away on a computer keyboard. He looks very fraught.

'You had a smooth journey here, did you?' He doesn't look up. Rude!

'Well,' I say, 'I can't answer that. One minute I'm drinking coffee in a café and talking to this fellow sat opposite, and the next, pouf! I'm at your reception desk, feeling thoroughly lost and not a little silly.'

They look at each other and smile knowingly. You know, I'm beginning to wonder if this could be some kind of sales pitch.

'You're not *Time Share* are you?' I've raised my voice. Don't often do that unless pushed. 'You're not trying to sell me a holiday home here, I hope, because my wife and I always go to the same hotel in Southport, every year.' Well, her mother's in Southport.

'No, Michael, we're not selling anything,' says the second one. I do like that silk white shirt he's wearing.

'The young man you spoke of, *he* brought you to this place. Oriel, that's his name. He works for us and is one of our trusted messengers.'

'That man in the café? Brought me here? Bloody kidnapped me, you mean!' I don't often swear, but I've had a long day. Meetings all morning, a working lunch, an afternoon wading through paperwork, then to cap it all, this Oriel chappy landing me in blooming no-mans-land. Well, I mean, how would you feel?

'Do you mind telling me where I am and why I'm here?' I say, stepping up the volume. This benign attitude of theirs is killing me. I'd rather have an all out row.

'You're in the Kingdom of Gloria,' says the shirt man. 'The Roof of the World.'

'Gloria? Roof of the World?' I say: 'Never heard of them.' Well, I'm not one for foreign travel.

'We are representatives of one of our most senior and revered messengers,' he goes on. 'At present he is recruiting more staff. You and some other privileged beings, have been short-listed.'

'Short-listed for what?' I ask, and sit up nice and straight.

'To work with us, of course.'

'With you?' Now I straighten my tie. Well, you never know.

'We are in the process of interviewing people in their fifties: men of good character, with life's experience, who possess managerial skills and bear our senior messenger's most esteemed name.'

'Which is?'

'Michael. His name is Michael, same as yours.'

'Well,' I say, 'My mother chose my name. I'd nothing to do with it. And I didn't know I was on any list.'

Have I been head-hunted then? Now, there's a thought. I'm not a proud man but the idea does appeal. And it would impress Rita.

'It's kind of you to consider me,' I say, ironing my tone, 'but as you are most probably aware, I already hold a managerial post in a reputable London insurance company.'

'You could keep your day job,' says the computer man, peering up at me from under bushy white brows, 'This would be more of a part-time post. More ... undercover, you understand?'

'What does your Michael do?'

I'm beginning to warm to the idea. Undercover? Mm. I've always fancied being a bit of a Dick Barton.

'Michael is the Prince of the Celestial Armies, commanded by God to drive the rebel angels out of Gloria.'

Celestial Armies! Rebel angels! Well, I never!

'You have many rebels, do you?' I ask. Well, I always thought that angels were all good.

'We've more than we can currently handle,' says the shirt man, adjusting his white cuffs. 'And what is more, our numbers are increasing. By recruiting more aids, we hope to remedy this unfortunate, and potentially dangerous problem.'

'Angels exist here and on earth, you know, Michael,' says the computer man. 'Some are shining examples of goodness and light, while others tend to wander off the path. And that's where *you* would come in.'

'How? In what way would I come in?'

'Your job would be to monitor the angels in your district and report back to us.'

'I didn't know we had any angels in Monkton Priors,' I say. 'My wife's an angel, of course.'

I laugh, trying to inject a bit of humour into the proceedings; but they stare back stony faced.

'Each of our successful candidates will be allocated his area,' says the shirt man. 'Monkton Priors would be yours. We have drawn lists of every human angel currently living on earth. These must be monitored and assessed on a regular basis. If you wish to see the figures, I have them all on database.'

'But why bother with all this?' I ask. I've pulled up the collar of my overcoat. Haven't they heard of central heating?

'We need to ensure that earthly angels do not fall by the wayside, of course,' says the computer man. 'Wings come at a price, Michael. Adopting this method saves us a lot of trouble when these beings eventually pass over.'

'Into Gloria, you mean?'

'Correct.'

'You see, Michael,' says the shirt man, 'if reports show that a human angel has dropped below our minimum standards, the moment they come to us, they are reassessed, sent for re-habilitation then found appropriate positions within our celestial hierarchy.'

'Surveillance,' continues the computer man, tapping away at the keys, 'reduces the risk of a major rebellion.'

He leans forward in his seat and fixes me with sharp brown eyes. 'And we do not want another of those.'

They shake their heads, look glum and rise slowly to their feet.

End of interview. As they move in silence from behind the table, I notice that each of them is wearing a pair of wings. The shirt man has the nicest: layers of long, thick, creamy feathers, reaching up to a point.

'We will let you know of our decision in due course,' he says, displaying gleaming, white teeth. He's got it all, that one.

'But how?' I ask. 'How will I know?'

He smiles benignly. 'You will. You will know.'

They bow. I bow. I'm getting the hang of this now and am about to ask them how to get home when an icy wind thumps me in the back, sweeps me off my feet and zaps me into space - Wham! I'm out for the count. Next thing I know, I'm standing inside my front gate. All the lights in our house are out. Funny that. I glance at my watch: Ten o'clock at night! Good Lord! I've been away all that time. Perhaps Rita's got up a search party, or gone to bed early. No, she'd wait up for me, I'm sure of that.

I let myself in and sit on the bottom stair to catch my breath and re-adjust my gyros. That's when I see the note propped against the telephone: my name on the envelope in Rita's firm hand writing.

I won't draw this next bit out, or go on about feelings: disappointment, betrayal and such like; I might get a bit emotional and I don't want to do that. But in a word, she's gone. Left me and run off with the furniture restorer. I had my suspicions all along, to be honest. Well, how many weeks does it take to French polish a coffee table?

What a day! I crawl, literally crawl upstairs and into my bed and despite all that's happened, sleep like a log, even without Rita's back to keep me warm.

Next morning, early, there's a ring at the door. Rita! Rita! Could it be? I fling off the bedclothes - put on my dressing gown - trip over my slippers, take the stairs two at a time, heart pounding, hands shaking. I grope for the key, unlock the front door and fling it open. No-one! No Rita. Not a dickey bird! Well, only George, our milkman delivering his round whistling away, bright and breezy as usual.

'Morning!'

'Morning!'

There's the clink of bottles, the hum of early morning traffic, the promise of skies clearing after a heavy rain storm. I stand in a puddle, with my dressing gown half on half off, disappointment stabbing at my guts. Then I notice something lying on the side of the step. A parcel! A large, square parcel wrapped in nice, smooth brown paper. Let's see. No stamp; just my name scrawled in large fancy lettering across the front. It could be Christmas. Who am I kidding? If Rita were here, it would be. She loves surprises, does Rita. I take off layer after layer. And next, tissue paper, layer after layer of that too. Whatever could it be? I couldn't recall ordering anything. Finally, a large cardboard box presents itself. I lift the lid.

Wings! A pair of angel's wings! Not as nice as the shirt man's, I grant you, but wings nonetheless. Well, I never! What did they mean by giving me wings? Did it mean I had got the job? Was I expected to fly off to Gloria or what? 'You'll know.' Isn't that what they said? But did I?

I bet it was Oriel who had brought the parcel. So where was he then?

'Are you there, Oriel? No need to hide. I won't bite.'

I look down the side passage and in the wheelie bin. Nothing. And yet the strange thing is I feel better and I'm peckish too. There's a nice bit of lean bacon in the fridge, and eggs. Yes, that would do nicely.

I gaze up at the sky: one last look before turning to go indoors. I think of all that has happened: finding myself in a strange land, meeting those angels, being zapped back to earth and discovering Rita gone ... all that and now it would seem an offer of a job! I wonder about Rita, of having thought her my angel for so long, over all those married years. She's still my angel though, even after what's happened. So much known, so much unknown, so much changed. Experiences must count for something mustn't they? Some new part put into us. No, I don't think I'll accept the post - never fancied being a monitor at school, let alone of Monkton Priors. And I never much cared for heights. Wings or no wings, bad things or good, own or disown them, it's being human, being fallible, free to make our choices that matter in the end. And I don't think I'd have it any other way.

The rain is just a drizzle now and touches of blue are starting to peep through the clouds. But best of all there is a rainbow: one huge multicoloured arc reaching right across the sky.

The sun is finally shining through the rain.

A SEASONAL TALE

We've been mates for years, Dave and me: met at teachers training college - the students union it was, and stayed friends ever since. Once a year we meet up for a couple of jars at my local pub. It's the only chance we have, since he teaches up north and me down south. Poles apart you might say. And yet we get on really well. Come Christmas, and there we are, regular as clockwork propping up the bar at The Bear Inn and jawing away over our pints of best bitter. He comes south to visit his old Aunt Bea. 'Ninety but nifty', is how he describes her.

He can tell a yarn or two can Dave when he's in the mood. I never thought he had a sensitive side though, 'til last year. But when he told this tale I changed my mind. Folk can be deep and as my mother always said, 'Nothing is as it seems.' Well, it certainly wasn't in this case. Here's his story. Make of it what you will.

The thought of spending Christmas in Uncle Bertram's draughty barn, turned me right off. But Aunt Bea's been good to me and to tow the line this once and spend a couple of days with her and her brother, was probably no bad thing.

I packed my ancient Morris Minor, and armed with a flask of steaming coffee and a rug for Auntie's knees, we headed north in the direction of Little Compton Underwood.

It was after we'd left the arterial road that things started to get difficult. The lanes grew increasingly narrow and winding as we drove further and further off the beaten track. Then we hit a small junction with no signpost. It was getting dark and the lane flanked by high hedges, made it look even darker. To cap it all my car suddenly gave an almighty shudder and stalled. I tried to restart but with no luck. Oh God! I thought. Please don't let's be stranded here in the middle of nowhere. My heart lurched as I glanced at the petrol gauge. Empty! Empty? But there *was* fuel in the tank. I remembered filling up at my local garage.

Aunt Bea shot me one of her glances, pursed her lips and reached for the coffee flask. At least I'd got something right! I said that I'd find the nearest house and see if they'd any spare petrol they could let me have. Her eyebrows shot up in horror.

'Do you mean to say that you don't carry extra fuel in case of emergency, David?'

My silence told her that I didn't. I felt really bad as we sat there waiting for the engine to cool so that I could look inside it, although what I expected to find, I'd no idea. It's amazing how inertia can blot out those little necessities. To tell the truth, I'd rather have been doing anything than going to Uncle Bertram's freezing mansion.

There was no luck in the engine department, so I took an empty petrol can from the boot and asked Auntie if she'd be all right if I left her for a bit. I hated the idea but what else could I do? She was too old and frail to walk any distance. But she assured me that she'd be fine and for me not to worry. She isn't a bad old stick, you know. Under that frosty front of hers, she's got a heart of gold.

I handed Auntie the rug from the back seat and set off down the lane. It was growing darker and colder now - that horrid damp chill that seeps into your bones. A recent downpour had made the ground muddy and it was slippery underfoot. Apart from a few sheep in a neighbouring field there was nothing really: Just the quiet emptiness of the countryside on a bleak day in the middle of winter.

Then I saw in the distance, a large open field and a stone farmhouse with lights. Boy! Was I relieved. On Christmas Eve, lost and cold, there's no more comforting, or welcoming sight I can tell you.

I climbed over a broken gate, crossed the sodden grass and eventually found myself in a small cobbled yard. A dog barked in the distance but there was no sign of it.

I stumbled up to the front door, put my can on the stone step and pulled a rusty bell chain. Before you could say, 'Merry Christmas!' the door swung open and this gorgeous looking woman stood there. She was a stunner! Terrific figure, the sort you dream about and long blonde wavy hair. But what struck me most, was the light and warmth of the room beyond. There was a small group of men and women standing around talking. The men wore dinner jackets and the women were in long evening dresses. It was really weird. I mean who wears all that stuff nowadays? The woman who'd opened the door to me, was in red velvet and smoked a cigarette through a gold holder.

She called to the others: 'He's here!' as though they'd been expecting me. I told them they must have muddled me up with someone else, but they just smiled and shook their heads.

'I think there's been some mistake,' I said. But they just laughed and shook their heads some more. It was really unnerving.

The blonde-haired woman closed the front door softly behind me. I swung round. Wow, that's it, I thought. I'm their prisoner now. She took my arm and told me not to be nervous, that I was very welcome and it was kind of me to have come. Her voice was creamy and quiet, almost hypnotic so that for a moment I felt myself almost sucked into the situation.

One of the male guests took my overcoat whilst another placed a whiskey in my hand.

'Have this before we begin,' he said.

Begin? Begin what?

I thought of Aunt Bea sitting alone in the car getting colder by the minute and me, standing there like a jerk with my mouth open.

'Please,' I insisted. 'If I could just explain, I'm not who you think I am. There's been some mistake, some misunderstanding.'

But they just smiled some more. One or two of them laughed but not in an unkind way.

'Now,' said the woman, 'where would you like us?'

What the Dickens was she on about? I must have looked completely out of it, because she asked me again:

'Where would you like us dear?'

My God! I thought. My life's slipping out of control; losing the way, running out of petrol and now this. These people are mad or I am. It occurred to me then that perhaps they thought I was some kind of cabaret; a song and dance act or a strip o' gram perhaps. Imagine stripping to that lot and with my size, I thought. This made me smile, and I relaxed a bit. Although I was freaked out by it all, there was something about them I liked. One thing was sure, I couldn't leave until I'd done what they'd wanted, whatever that was. Not to do so would disappoint, anger even. For some reason I mattered to them. It was strange - the whole set up was strange, and yet I wasn't scared, simply puzzled.

Right, I thought. I'd better get cracking or I'll never get out of here. The most natural thing to do, it seemed, was to invite the guests to sit down; which I did. Candles were brought, lit and placed on an old upright piano in the corner of the room.

I will always remember that sight: the small collection of men and women, some sitting on armchairs, others on the floor - the women with diamonds sparkling at their throats, the shadowed beams stretching across the low ceilinged room and the hush, as they waited all eyes on me. I heard the owls outside, a clock ticking, logs burning in the grate and the warmth all around me.

And suddenly my mind cleared. It was as though a curtain had lifted and all was revealed. I knew now what it was I had to do.

'There was a child born in Bethlehem,' I said, and began to tell the Christmas Story. Well, you could have knocked me over with a feather. I'm not religious by a long chalk. And yet here I was telling them about Jesus, Mary and Joseph; the stable and the visiting shepherds. They listened like no-one's ever listened to me before, certainly not in the classroom, that's for sure. All eyes were on my face, drinking in the words. When I'd finished, there was a pause, a few coughs and a bit of shuffling as they rose to their feet. They shook my hand in turn and thanked me before turning to talk among themselves. They spoke of the Christ Child and what the birth meant to them. I was no longer the centre of attention. My job was done. Finished. I'd simply told my story ... been the narrator as it were.

I said my goodbyes and they all thanked me again, and the woman who'd let me in, now quite happily and willingly opened the door and let me out. The laughter, the chatter switched off like a radio. There was no more light, no warm fire but a wall of black and silence and the return to cold.

I took out my torch, stumbled over the yard, crossed the field and climbed the gate back onto the lane. Thoughts of Aunt Bea returned with a vengeance. Was she all right? How long had I been gone, for goodness' sake? I peered at my watch. It had stopped. And another thing; in my haste to leave, I'd forgotten to pick up the blooming petrol can, let alone ask for fuel.

I ran like fury along the lane to the car. And there was Auntie, bless her, sitting bolt upright in the driving seat now. Puffing and blowing I said how sorry I was to have taken so long.

'Nonsense. You were only twenty minutes. Jump in!'

Twenty minutes? An hour, more like. I shook my watch, and found to my dismay that it had started again. She was right. I'd only been away for twenty minutes.

Too dazed to say more, I climbed into the passenger seat and Aunt Bea turned the ignition key. The Morris started first time. When I protested, she blamed a faulty petrol gauge. Well, you don't argue with Aunt Bea, not if you know what's good for you. So off we went, Auntie choosing the right fork and driving us to the nearest garage.

Well, we found our way quite easily after that and spent a tolerably pleasant Christmas at Uncle Bertram's. There was the usual sherry party and Uncle's overcooked turkey but he keeps a well stocked wine cellar with some pretty good stuff. I didn't tell them about my experience, there didn't seem much point really, and they wouldn't have believed me anyway.

'Is that the end?' I asked, picking up our empty glasses. It was my round.

'Not quite,' said Dave. 'Last summer I had to go to that part of the world on business. On a whim, I decided to do a detour and retrace my steps. I found the spot where my car had conked out and walked back to the same gate that I'd climbed to reach the house. I looked across the field expecting it to be there, but there was no sign of it.'

'No sign of that spooky house?'

'No. No building, no yard, nothing. I couldn't believe my eyes. I was so certain that I'd found the right spot. On the way back to the car I met a farm-hand, and asked him about the place. He said there hadn't been a house in that field since the Second World War. It had been bombed one Christmas Eve. Apparently, the owner, a young, wealthy divorcee, was throwing a house party at her family home when it happened. There was a tradition, you see, a custom going back many years that every December 24th a volunteer, often a stranger from one of the nearby villages, would visit the house and regale the Christmas Story. They'd be welcomed along with the other guests with warmth and generosity. But on Christmas Eve 1940, a German plane, making its way back to the coast, off loaded its bombs and one hit the house. Everyone was killed. The place remained a ruin for years. It was never rebuilt and eventually reverted to grassland.

'But what about the story teller?' I asked. 'Was he killed as well?'

'Luckily for him, it happened before he arrived. It seems that news of the bombing had reached the neighbouring villages. And so, of course, the fellow never set off.'

For some moments we said nothing, just sat gazing into our empty glasses. I shuddered. It was a strange story.

'It's as though for all those years they'd been waiting for you, expecting you,' I said at last.

'Maybe. Who knows? We'll never know. But perhaps in the end it didn't really matter who gave the Christmas Story. Not so long as it was told.'

SANGRIA

Roger always hated Saturday afternoons.

'Why?' I asked him. 'Why Saturday afternoons?'

'Nowt to do.'

'What about your girlfriend?'

'What about her?'

'Can't ya spend some time with *her*?'

'Maureen watches football, Saturdays.'

'Right.'

We sat in silence then - me and my mate. Sat and stared into our warm ales and nursed our dreams. Rog with his beaches, palm trees and sangria and me with my Lamborghini, hot totties and Monte Carlo.

'Ever fancied an adventure?' I asked, draining my glass.

'What sort of an adventure?'

'I don't know - must be one waiting for us somewhere.'

He cast hooded eyes around the half-empty bar. 'I can't see one.'

'Course you can't, idiot! You got to go looking. Adventures don't just drop into your lap. Got any dosh?'

'Nah, I'm skint.'

'No matter.' I rose to my feet. 'Come on! Let's get looking.'

And so we wandered up the high street that sunless afternoon without a penny piece between us - past the market place, with its stale fishy smells, past the charity shops and the town hall, past all the shoppers searching for this bargain or that, until we came to the church; a grey monstrous building - Victorian, I think - standing back a little from the road. I can't say I was sold on it, but Rog, without so much as a word, suddenly made a right, and hoofed it up the path to the main door. I saw him turn the handle but it was locked.

'What's up with you Rog?' I called puffing after him. 'Had a vision?'

'No.'

'What then?'

'I'm going t' belfry.'

'T' belfry! What for?'

'To ring bloody bells of course. What else?' Then he fished in his pocket and brought out his Leatherman tool.'

'What ya doing?' I gasped drawing up beside him.

'What d'ya think I'm doing?'

He released the awl and inserted it into the lock.

'You're mad! That's breaking and entering. You'll get done.'

'So what! You wanted an adventure.'

Normally he's a bit slow, is Rog. Sluggish is the word that comes to mind. This turn of events was nothing short of amazing. Well, I was all set to warn him about hell and damnation, when the vicar suddenly appeared beside us. It gave me quite a jolt, arriving at our sides unexpected like.

'May I help you?' he said, staring at the pen knife.

'Eh, well,' I spluttered, 'my friend here, he wants to have a look round your church.' I didn't mention bells.

'And you found it locked.'

His eyes were very old but clear … translucent almost.

'It's fortunate I came by then, isn't it?'

His face broke into a thousand wrinkles as he fixed us with a benign smile. 'Churches should never be locked. They belong to the people. You wouldn't like to be locked out of your house, would you now?'

The vicar wore a thick dog collar, a long black cassock, I think you call it, and had a couple of large keys hanging from round his waist. He took one of them, unlocked the door and turned the big round rusty handle.

'I'd be happy to show you around,' he twinkled, stepping aside to let us pass.

Well, I wasn't keen, but Rog looked fair wrapped.

'Cool!' he said. And could he have a gander at the belfry? I'd no idea he had a thing about bells.

'Put that tool away, will ya?' I hissed, as we followed the old man inside.

It was ever so dark, with a funny musty smell. I noticed plenty of lights hanging from the roof but the vicar didn't switch them on. Perhaps he was saving on electricity.

First off, he showed us the font. Made of stone it was, with carvings of angels and that, all along the sides. Then he took us to see this fierce looking eagle made of shiny brass with a thumping great Bible laid on top. And last but not least, we were shown the altar. That was real nifty, with a lovely embroidered cloth with lots of gold thread.

Well, there we were, standing on the altar steps, freezing cold, listening to this vicar droning on about the history of the place, and me thinking some adventure this was, when suddenly he let out a strangled cry, clutched his chest and fell in a heap at our feet.

Struth!

I turned on Rog. 'See what you done, coming in here?'

'I done nothing!' But I could see he was shaken. He knelt and placed his head against the old boy's heart.

'Well?' I said, 'Is there a beat?'

Rog stared at me, his eyes wide with terror. 'I think he's dead.'

'Bloody Hell! Know how to resuscitate?'

'No. Do you?'

'No.'

We stood rigid. It was awful! I shall never forget it, the gloom of the place. Some of the pews creaked but it was ever so quiet. And this cold chill all around like a great damp cloak.

'Get your mobile out,' I said.

He twice checked his pockets then bit his lip.

'What's up Rog?'

'Think I left it in't pub.'

'Idiot!'

'Use yours then, smarty pants.'

'Can't. It's at home.'

I thought a moment. 'Right. Tell you what we do. You stay with him. I'll go and find a phone box and ring for an ambulance. Okay?'

I ran down that aisle like the devil was at my heels. But when I reached the door, it was locked. I tried and tried to open it. I turned the handle over and over but to no avail. I just couldn't believe the thing wouldn't open. The vicar must have locked the door after us. But he'd said that he didn't believe in locking churches, so why would he? I pondered on this a moment then decided there was nothing for it, but to go back and take the key from round the old man's waist. I ran back up the aisle, trying to keep a cool head. But my heart was pounding and I felt sick. As I grew closer, I could sense that awful cold again, it seemed worse the further into the church you went. I shuddered and my teeth began to chatter.

When I reached the altar steps, I stopped short. Rog and the body had gone. Vanished! Nowhere to be seen.

I was going mad. Must be. First the locked door and now no body, and worse, no Rog. I looked in the choir stalls, the chapel, in the pulpit and even behind the altar, but there was no sign of them.

I searched, tripping over this and that in my haste. After a bit, I spotted a small wooden door in the side wall of a chapel. That was when the lights went on. I jumped as I felt a smart tap on the back. I swung round, my heart in my mouth. Standing over me, was a young man carrying a music case.

'You a guest?' he asked, breathing peppermint fumes over my face.

'A guest?' I said. 'I didn't know you needed an invitation to get in.'

'No! No!' His head wobbled precariously. 'A wedding guest.'

'No,' I said, staring at him blankly. 'I haven't been invited to any wedding.'

I stumbled after him as he strode over to the organ, opened his case, took out sheets of music, sat down and pulled out some stops.

'I just want to get out.' I felt very timid and small.

'There's a wedding in a few minutes.' He peered at me over his specs which were held together with elastoplast. 'How did you get in? The verger, was it?'

'No, not the verger - your vicar. *He* let us in ... me and me mate. Now I've lost me mate and ...'

'The vicar? You say the vicar let you in?'

Oh heck! He didn't know what had happened, and there was this service coming up and no one to marry the bride and groom.

'Our vicar's away.' He was frowning now. 'She won't be back 'til next week.'

'*She?*'

'Yes. Mary's on holiday. Our young locum's taking the service.'

'Young, you say young? Oh I don't think I would describe him as young.'

'Yes, yes. Recently ordained. Green around the gills, I'd say, but capable enough.'

'Then who was it that let us in?'

He pulled out some stops and played a series of loud chords like he was building up to something, before turning to face me. There was a bead of sweat over his thin upper lip.

'This vicar you speak of: was he old, dressed in a black cassock with keys hanging round his waist?'

I nodded. 'He showed us around. Friendly sort of a chap - knew his stuff.'

'So he should. He was parish parson for over fifty years.'

'*Was?*'

'The Reverend Edgar Poole died seventy years back. He's buried in our churchyard.'

An icy chill crept up my spine and I felt myself go weak at the knees.

'Yes,' he went on, 'The old man suffered a heart attack in this very church. He dropped dead by those altar steps. Apparently he'd been showing a couple like yourselves around when it happened. He's haunted our church for years, although I've never seen him I have to say.'

As I stood trying to take this all in, the church bells started up.

'Where's your belfry?' I asked, when I could find me tongue.

'You can't go up there now dear chap - not while they're playing for the wedding.'

'I must find me mate.' I was desperate.

He sighed, threw me a pitying look, pointed to an alcove covered by a green baize curtain, then turned his back on me and began to play.

A couple of minutes later, I was standing in a room of men and women pulling long red and cream striped bell ropes.

'Have you seen me mate, Roger?' I shouted, trying to make myself heard over the racket. They all looked at me funny like, and shook their heads. Oh, God! Things were going from bad to worse.

I ran back into church, past a couple of ushers who offered me a service sheet then out through the wide open door. There were photographers, bridesmaids, guests, all milling around like a lot of hens. But oh, it was that good to be in the fresh air again and out of that fusty, eerie building.

Then I saw him! Rog! He waved frantically as he pushed his way through the throng towards me.

'Where the heck have you been? Where's the body?' I cried, relief and rage flooding my arteries.

'Guess what?' said Rog, his eyes bright and beautiful.

'What?'

'I'm going to ring bells at a wedding.'

'Bit late for that,' I said, through gritted teeth.

'Not church bells - hand bells. One of the ringers hasn't turned up. They've asked me to take his place. Me!'

'You know nowt about hand bells.' I said, wanting to throttle him.

'Yes, I do. Learnt at school ... It was only thing I was good at.'

'I've been worried sick, and all you talk of is bells. Where's that vicar? What you done with him?'

'Calm down!' said Rog, waving to some girl tottering around in high heels. 'After you'd gone, and you were gone like it seemed ages, I heard noises in't belfry, so went up there and there were the ringers all getting ready to do their bit. I told them what had happened.' He gave a dopey smile. 'That's where I met Pauline. She was the one who asked me to help out and ring the hand bells.'

'Never mind her! Stick to the point, will ya!'

'No, but that is the point. She came with me, you see - back to the altar. But when we got there, he'd gone.'

'The old vicar?'

'Aye.'

'But he was dead.'

'Aye.'

'You're sure about that Rog?'

'That he'd gone? Course I'm sure. It gave me a heck of a jolt not seeing him lie there. But she told me not to fret - said it had happened before to visitors - to people like us.'

Well, it seems that Pauline had told him more or less what the organist had told me. It was a relief to hear his side of things, I can tell you, and I relaxed a bit after that, enough anyway, to sit in on the service and listen to Rog play his blooming hand bells. He was good an' all.

They play all over now, him and Pauline, and Saturday afternoons are Rog's busiest time. They're having their own wedding soon. Well, he never did have much in common with Maureen.

Strange how things turn out. But I reckon that without his best mate to look after him, he'd still be sitting in that pub, staring into his ale and dreaming of beaches, palm trees and sangria.

SOMETHING UNSPOKEN

'I wonder,' Alfred remarked, slicing his buttered toast into soldiers, 'Might you have sent them to be laundered, do you suppose?'

'No, I do not suppose,' snapped George, tapping into his boiled egg. 'What would be the point of sending the bottoms without the top?'

Alfred looked benignly at his friend and shook his head. He had heard things, unkind things about George and his weak bladder.

'Well,' he said, adding a note of feeble cheer to his voice, 'I daresay your pyjama bottoms will turn up sooner rather than later.' And then turning to the adjacent table, 'Where are we off to this cold winter's morning? Any ideas, Miss Darling?'

'It's a surprise,' she replied in a stage whisper. 'We're to meet in the hall at ten-thirty. Didn't you read the notice board, Mr Pepperton?' And she lowered her head pretending to be cross.

'I expect we'll be conveyed in that monstrous Range Rover of his,' George barked, throwing down his egg spoon with a clatter. 'It takes all my strength to climb into that wretched old wagon. Quite unsuitable for old people, but Jeremy will act the country squire.'

'Oh, please keep your voice down Mr Winterbourne, he may hear you,' she urged, gathering her knitting and stuffing it into a tapestry bag.

'And how you manage Miss Darling with that sciatica of yours, I'll never know,' he continued, pleasurably fuelled by her agitation.

'We enjoy our outings,' she sparked, watching Alfred abandon his breakfast and tiptoe out of the room, 'And if Jeremy didn't take us, then who would?'

'Quite so.' George winked broadly in a bid to make up. 'Any clues as to where we're going, Miss Darling?'

'I have a sneaking suspicion we may be taken to Wellingford House Hotel for coffee and cream cakes. Very nice.' And noting the detached look on his face, 'If you do decide to join us, Mr Winterbourne, then I think it will only be the three of us: you, Mr Pepperton and myself. Oh, and Jeremy of course, that makes four doesn't it? Silly me!'

His fingers played with the sugar bowl. 'Mrs Rushton not coming?'

'Evelyn has a prior engagement,' she replied stiffly.

George felt a pang of disappointment. He liked Evelyn. No, damn it, he loved her. Fine bones, long legs, cut glass accent and a smart warm manner: that was Evelyn. Not popular with the other old ducks though. No, she was more of a man's woman. Give her a good political bone to chew and she was away. Top drawer too. Cheltenham Ladies College, Oxford University, and her old man had been something big in the army. No wonder Jeremy liked having her around the place: he positively sought her out when prospective clients came to visit. 'Ah, here's our Mrs Rushton,' he'd say, ushering guests into the recently refurbished day room. And there the residents would sit, but it was Evelyn who was singled out for comments. Charming loveable Evelyn, relaxing by the fire in twin set and pearls, the jacket of her *Hermes* suite draped casually round her shoulders, a copy of *The Tatler* in her lap, a glass of *Bristol Cream* sherry at her side and a radiant smile on her face. What better advertisement for Lampton Court? She sparkled like a bottle of bubbly on a cold winter's night. Magic.

It was yesterday he'd made his decision. He'd ask her to marry him. George knew he was a rough diamond, self-made from humble begin-nings but so what? They got on well and made each other laugh. A year ago it was, that he'd first set eyes on her eating dinner with her friend, Miss Darling. One look between them and George knew she was the one. All those years making his pile in the car industry; holidaying on the continent, in the States and Hong Kong, and he'd never met a woman after his own heart. He'd had his share, of course but there'd not been one he'd fancied enough to marry. Now in his twilight years, he'd found her. And after all, if she were to accept, it wouldn't be such an upheaval for either of them. They could move away from this house, and that fluttery Miss Darling who was always hanging about, over to the married quarters, those converted stables over by the paddock. One of the couples had recently died, so there'd doubtless be a vacancy.

George started to get up, tugging at the corners of the white linen tablecloth to steady himself. He bid Lucy Darling good morning and made his way into the Georgian hall with its gracious windows that looked out over large lawns, full of the trees he loved so much. He shouldn't complain. Lampton Court was expensive, some would say ostentatious, with Jeremy's penchant for grey hounds, real and china, the family coat of arms stuck up in every room, and a distant claim to royalty. But at least he took them out from time to time, and saw they were given their medical checks. George gave a long sigh. It was no fun growing old, having to leave your pad and sell up your possessions to pay for the last few years of life.

He mounted the wide, sweeping staircase taking each step slowly and carefully. He didn't want a fall at his time of life: falls presaged the end for so many. Dependency. He hated it. After a lifetime of bachelor freedom, it was more than he could stomach having to lay himself open to those bossy carers, who treated them all like children with half a brain. And now he had this bother of a problem. Blast it! And with Evelyn in the picture too. It wasn't that he didn't want to go on the outings Jeremy organised, more that he was scared. Yes, that was the truth of it. What if he couldn't make it in time? Another accident he dreaded. Public lavatories were few and far between particularly in department stores as he'd learned to his great cost.

He stopped in his tracks, felt the heat slowly diffuse his neck and face. Beads of sweat prickled his brow and he began to sway. For it to have happened even that once, was bad enough but in front of all those shoppers! That warm rush of water filling his underpants, running scalding down his legs and forming a disgusting pool at his feet.

'You all right, Mr Winterbourne?'

George stifled a sob. Trina! Trust her to find him like this. She'd have him wear a potty round his neck, if she knew. Lucky for him that incident happening when it did. At least then he was free to disappear off home. Whereas now ...

'Why don't you use the stair lift, Mr Winterbourne? That's what it's there for,' she scolded, her pink nylon overall straining across a fat, matronly breast.

'Because while my legs can function, I shall use them, thank you, Trina.'

His rope-veined hand clutched the banister, as he felt that undisciplined damp seeping into his trousers. One step and he'd be for it. A flood he dreaded more than death. Bugger these carers, forever interfering. His breaths were coming in gasps now and he felt dizzy. He must stay calm. If he stood still a few moments, the urge to pass water might subside enough for him to move on. He could sense Trina standing there, waiting: her moon face closed with authority and position.

'There's no need to stay, thank you. I can manage.'

'I'll send the lift up to you, Mr Winterbourne. We don't want you fainting on us.'

'Leave me!'

'Obstinate old fool,' he heard her mutter, as she walked on.

George waited until she was out of earshot before continuing his climb. He should have this problem seen to, he knew that, but to admit to this humiliating complaint was more than he could face. He recalled with shame, the whacks he'd received from his father for bed wetting as a boy, and once he'd soiled himself while playing Joseph in the school's nativity play.

Reaching the landing, he edged his way along the corridor, past Miss Little's room: the entrance blocked as usual by her walking frame, and dotty Ivy Parker's, who never knew what time of day it was, until in the distance, he saw the familiar gleam of his cream gloss painted door.

It was later, while searching in his drawer for a clean pair of underpants that he noticed his mislaid pyjama bottoms lying folded at the foot of his bed, washed, pressed and ready to wear.

Formerly an eighteenth century rectory, Wellingford House Hotel was set amidst acres of formal gardens and parkland.

The convivial receptionist conducted the little party into the busy coffee lounge, where there was a welcoming fire. Oriental rugs scattered the fine wooden floor and reproduction antiques were set in high relief against the pale peach walls.

'Look! There's Evelyn!' exclaimed Miss Darling, pointing to an elegantly suited woman, sitting in the far corner of the room.

'Where?' George fumbled for his glasses and put them on. Good God! So it was! Looking pretty all right too. And who, he'd like to know, was that man sitting with her?

He struck out at Miss Darling. 'You said she wasn't coming.'

'I didn't think she'd be here, Mr Winterbourne. What a coincidence.'

Coincidence be damned!

The waiter ushered them towards the bay window and comfortable armchairs while Jeremy, exclaiming on every aspect of the place, threw out his arms as though to embrace the entire estate.

'Is that white deer I can see over by the lake?' he cried. 'Wonderful!'

Stupid bugger! thought George, parking himself next to Alfred. Jeremy must surely have spotted Evelyn, why didn't he say something.

He prodded him in the thigh. 'Seen whose sitting over there?'

'Yes, Mr Winterbourne, I've seen.'

'Well, shouldn't we go over and join them?'

'I don't think that would be a good idea.'

'Why not?'

'Because we might be intruding.' And brightly to the others, 'Coffee and cream cakes everyone?'

George scowled: watched with disgust the others sinking their teeth into meringues and chocolate éclairs. The thought of food made him sick to the stomach, a stomach already churned up by what he'd seen. Evelyn with another man! Why hadn't she told him? And Jeremy! What was up with him? It was quite obvious he'd known she was going to be here. And that Darling woman: he'd a feeling she knew too. George sat silent while the others chatted. There was something going on and he'd like to know what. Several times he turned and stared angrily at Evelyn but she didn't respond, intent only on her companion. Deep in conversation they were.

Just when he thought he could bear it no longer, the two of them rose and threaded their way towards the door.

Now Jeremy jumped up, spilling coffee in his eagerness to reach them before they left. He shook the man warmly by the hand. So they knew each other ay? But hang on! George recognised him too. Lampton Court. Yes, he'd seen him not once but twice at Lampton Court and on both occasions he'd been talking to Jeremy. Was he planning to live there, George wondered? Had Evelyn worked her charm on him too? He certainly qualified for a place: elderly, well dressed, obviously moneyed. But there was nothing frangible about this chap. His step was steady, confident and there was a glamour about him that made George uneasy.

Evelyn turned to him and gave a little wave but before George had a chance to wave back, the two of them had swept out, leaving Jeremy in buoyant mood, eager to pay the bill and leave also.

On the return journey it started to snow. Thick flakes caused the wipers to work overtime and the little party to chime and exclaim their delight and apprehension. Any chance of opening the topic of Evelyn and her friend was lost and once back at the house, George, tired and depressed, retired to his room, where he spent the rest of the day and evening.

That night, he wet the bed. But it was not until morning that he awoke to the feel of a cold sodden mattress. He lay motionless, a child again, vulnerable and afraid. What would they do to him? Wet underpants you could wash yourself and pyjama bottoms, if you were quick off the mark, but a bed?

George got up and threw back the covers. There it was, the watery patch but not looking half as bad as it had felt. He thought for a moment before reaching for his worn hot water bottle at the foot of the bed. With shaking hands he unscrewed the cork and emptied most of the contents down the sink. Then puncturing the rubber with a sewing needle that he kept handy, he lay the bottle along with a strongly worded note on the bedside table. That should fox 'em, he thought, as he washed, dressed and went downstairs for a late breakfast.

He found Evelyn sitting on her own in the dining room reading the newspaper, a cup of coffee by her side.

'I'm sorry I appeared unsociable, yesterday morning ...' she began, indicating the chair next to her.

'It's your affair,' he sulked, sitting down heavily. 'I have no wish to interfere.'

'Oh, stop being so stuffy, George. I was having coffee with my solicitor.' She fixed him with that inquisitive gaze he'd grown to love. 'I couldn't come over and chat - it was business. Tedious, but necessary. How extraordinary all of us landing up at the same hotel like that.'

He sighed with relief. Solicitor, of course!

'My late husband's solicitor, actually,' she added, as though reading his thoughts. 'I wanted to make certain alterations, codicils to my will.'

'I did wonder,' pursued George, feeling almost festive as he ordered coffee and toast. 'Only I thought I'd seen him here a couple of times.'

'You will have done.' She brushed crumbs from her lap with long sweeping movements. 'Anyway,' her voice was suddenly edgy, nervous, 'thank goodness, things are finally settled and I can move from here with peace of mind.'

Move? What did she mean by move?

'Don't look so shocked, George. You know I don't fit in at Lampton Court.'

He banged his fist on the table. 'Rot! Jeremy adores you. You're an asset to the place, Evelyn, and you know it.'

'The other women don't think so. They're hardly my type nor I theirs.'

'But I don't understand. I thought you were happy here. And you have Miss Darling. What about her? You get on with her.' Not forgetting me, he wanted to add.

Her lips tightened. 'Ah yes, Lucy.' She rolled her napkin and placed it into its ring.

He paused, watching, waiting for her to tell him.

'I'm going to live with my son,' she said finally.

'Your son? You never told me you had a son.'

'No, George. But there were reasons for that.'

Again, he waited. His heart heavy with hurt.

'When I was married to Leo, I had an affair. It was brief and passionate and we were reckless. I became pregnant. After Tim was born I put him up for adoption because my husband, although prepared to overlook and forgive the affair, didn't want to bring up the child as his own son. And that was the only way in those days that we could have respectfully got away with it.'

'But why didn't you tell me, Evelyn?' He felt sick, miserable, betrayed.

'It was too painful. Can't you understand that? Perhaps not. You've never been married with children.'

She gazed out of the window, at the grey morning mist and the post boy walking up the drive. 'Six months ago, Tim contacted me out of the blue. He wanted us to meet. For the first time since I'd given him up as a baby, we were to see each other. I can't begin to describe the feeling. I had let him go, given him away and yet he still wanted me, wanted me back. After all that time and despite his loving adoptive parents, he wanted to see me, his real mother. This young man of thirty-four rang me here, asked to meet and I agreed. I was terribly nervous, you can imagine. What picture did he hold of me in his head? But I needn't have worried. It was wonderful! He looked like me too and we got along so well. There was no resentment on his part, none whatsoever. I'm still amazed at his acceptance. Humbled by it. We've seen each other regularly since. Oh, George! Don't look so horrified. Everyone has secrets, you know. Even you.'

'Not from you Evelyn. Never.'

'No?' Her lips lifted at the corners and he felt himself redden.

'Is Tim married?'

She threw back her head and laughed. 'I wouldn't dream of living with a married son. Of course, one day he may be. But it won't involve me. Not by then.'

George stared at his untouched toast, too depressed to ask what she meant.

'I'll be living in Worcester,' she went on. 'You must come for visits. Come with Lucy. Tim can collect you both in the morning and bring you back in the evening in time for dinner.'

Like the laundry, he thought bitterly, I am to be collected and returned.

'Marry me, Evelyn,' he said, knowing already her answer.

She stared at him as though he'd asked her to jump off the Eiffel Tower.

'We could live in the married quarters. We'd be away from the house and have a bit of independence and you could visit your son as often as you liked. What do you say?'

She bowed her head, her voice barely audible.

'What a kind offer George.'

'Kind, be damned! I love you woman.'

'Thank you. I am very flattered. But you know that at our age ... No please allow me to finish,' as he raised his hand in protest. 'At our age it may not, probably wouldn't work. I'm used to being on my own now and you have always remained single. We are both far too old.'

'At least think about it, please?'

'No, George. I'm sorry. My decision is final.'

She licked lips that were dry and pale. And George noticed with a start how drawn she looked.

'Now,' she said, pushing back her chair, her manner pleasantly firm. 'How about a game of rummy tomorrow evening? Do say you'll join us. It would be just the three of us: You, Lucy and myself.'

George sat hunched and still, anger and hurt co-mingling. He had been dismissed. Like a child, his request had been turned down and now he was to be fobbed off with a small treat - a game of blasted rummy.

George found her, late that evening. Muffled in scarves and wearing his thick overcoat, he'd taken an after dinner walk in the moonlit garden, treading with care the luminous snow, gleefully conscious of the telling off he could expect on his return. Let them all bark, what did he care? He had to get out, away from prying eyes and ears, to curse and to cry, mindful that nothing could change Evelyn's intractable spirit. He'd lost her and not to another man either but to her son.

As he neared the vegetable plot he saw three feet in front of him what looked like a small upturned snowman. Dressed in her white mink coat and black brimmed hat, Miss Darling lay on her back quietly moaning.

'It's my ankle, Mr Winterbourne,' she whispered, as he hurried to her side. 'I slipped on some ice and I've sprained my ankle, and can't get up.'

'Doctor Clifford's on his rounds,' he panted, removing his overcoat and covering her. What was she doing out so late? It was unlike her to take walks even on hot days. He smiled to himself. Might she too nurse a longing, a secret, or a broken heart? He couldn't imagine the old girl in love. But it took all sorts, he supposed.

'You hang on there,' he said, clumsily patting her head. 'I'll raise the alarm and call Evelyn.'

'No!' She clutched his arm. 'Not Evelyn, please!'

He startled at her vice-like grip. Perhaps they'd had a tiff. Always together, the two of them - unhealthy, if you asked him.

'I'll be off then. We'll have you rescued in a jiffy, don't you worry,' George said cheerily, shaking a flurry of snow from his trouser bottoms.

'Thank you so much, Mr Winterbourne. How fortunate that you found me.'

Yes, he thought, hurrying as fast as he dare across the lawn. If I hadn't, you certainly wouldn't have made it through the night old girl.

A few were gathered outside to see Evelyn off. The more senior resident ladies sat in the day room and waved whenever they thought she was looking. Miss Darling, tapestry bag over one arm and walking with the aid of a stick, presented her with a scarf she'd especially knitted. The two of them stood close and whispered a good deal. Alfred had gone to visit his sister in Cheltenham, and George, pressed for some little momento to give Evelyn, had persuaded him to part with his book of Shakespearean sonnets.

Now Evelyn was by his side, speaking rapidly, seeking reassurances.

'I hate goodbyes George. You will come and visit. Promise?'

He feared her tacit gaze, watched instead the cab driver load her luggage into the boot. No son to pick her up? Ah, well. He'd never meet him now. Perhaps that was as it should be.

He kissed her cheek: felt that soft translucent skin peculiar to the old. 'I'll write,' he said, but knew he wouldn't.

Jeremy was next, threatening future treats: summer picnics, theatre outings, a concert at the cathedral. Organised events for the Lampton Court residents, no doubt, but coming from his lips, devised especially for her. What was it about Evelyn that inspired such a tractable desire to please? Jeremy seemed as much a victim as himself to that refutable charm of hers dispensed readily and with such eagerness, impenitent of the consequences.

'And are you recovering well, Miss Darling?' George asked, after they had waved Evelyn off and were making their way back to the house.

'Quite well, thank you Mr Winterbourne. Doctor Clifford has prescribed rest, but I had to come downstairs to say goodbye to my friend. It is always a loss, when one of us leaves.' Her grey eyes clouded. 'You were so kind helping me the other night. I am very grateful.'

'My pleasure,' returned George, permitting himself a small bow. 'It must have been pretty scary lying out there in the dark.'

'It was and I am not very brave. We all have our frailties do we not, Mr Winterbourne?'

He nodded, remembering the rest of that night. His alerting the staff and leading Doctor Clifford to where Miss Darling lay. Of them carrying her back to the house, covering her with blankets and giving her hot sweet tea. But it was the praise he remembered most. Praise for him. The carers, the doctor, and Jeremy all telling him he was a jolly good chap, finding her as he'd done, and so unselfish, covering her with his overcoat and reporting straight back. And wasn't it lucky that he he'd taken his walk when he did? Questions, admonishments all seemingly forgotten in the wake of Miss Darling's accident. It was a good feeling, a strange feeling to be singled out and commended.

At ten-thirty, he'd mounted the stairs with a light step and a warm heart. It was a little later, after George had undressed, washed, soaked his dentures and climbed into bed that he felt the rubber sheet under him. He lay quite still in the darkness, his heart banging against his chest. With everything happening he'd quite forgotten the bed wetting episode, the hot water bottle and the note he'd written. Switching on his bedside light, he turned back the bed clothes. There it was, large and square: brown and brutish and sour smelling. Then he spotted on a nearby table, a pack of incontinence pads and a note from Trina, with strong orders to wear one each night before retiring.

He'd been found out. All the joy went out of him. What now? If he continued to wet the bed, he might be sent to a nursing home and that would spell the beginning of the end for George. There was nothing for it. He'd have to wear those wretched nappies and be a baby all over again.

His mind switched now to Miss Darling limping towards the day room. 'Such a brave woman,' she was saying. 'So uncomplaining.'

What did she mean, brave, uncomplaining? She indicated two wing chairs for them to sit down.

'Evelyn hid her frailties very well, Mr Winterbourne. That was why she sometimes appeared a little, how shall I say, over ebullient?'

Her loose lidded eyes were cold with the contempt she no longer took pains to hide. 'Evelyn asked me to tell you after she had gone. Now is a suitable time, I think.'

'Tell me what, Miss Darling?'

'She is dying.'

He stared. What was she saying?

'I'm sorry to be the bearer of bad tidings. Cancer is an emotive subject and affects people in different ways. She did not wish to discuss it, you understand. Not even with you, Mr Winterbourne. We decided it was for the best.'

His lips trembled. 'We?'

'Evelyn and I. Jeremy and Doctor Clifford knew, of course, but kept it from the residents.'

Anger filled his throat. What right had she to this awful secret?

'Tell me something Miss Darling. Why didn't Tim collect her today?'

'He was busy with patients,' she said, hugging the tapestry bag close.

'Come to the point, Miss Darling.'

'Tim is manager of Trinity House Nursing Home. That is where she's gone to spend her last months. A nursing home in Worcester.'

George sat silent. So absorbed had he been in his own world, he'd failed to mark the changes, the tell tale signs of illness. Had she trusted him enough to share her joy and her sorrow, could things have been different between them? Perhaps he had not deserved her after all.

'Evelyn and I arrived at Lampton Court within months of each other.' Miss Darling's eyes were bright with tears. 'I'd been looking after my sick mother until then. Ironic, isn't it? When she eventually died, it was time for *me* to be cared for. Evelyn and I became friends - close friends. There was nothing we hid from each other, no secrets we didn't share. Coming from similar backgrounds, we spoke the same language. So important in a friendship, don't you agree?' She agitated an amber ring on her little finger. 'And then you arrived. She didn't want a man, didn't need fussing around, adoring. Evelyn found your attention cloying, unpalatable. But you wouldn't take the hint, would you? Wouldn't leave her alone. And she was too kind, too well mannered to tell you.'

'I loved her, Miss Darling,' he said simply.

'And so did I, Mr Winterbourne.'

She unclasped the tapestry bag and withdrawing her knitting, set two balls of navy blue wool on the table in front of her.

'Anyway, it's Tim's turn now,' she said, rapidly casting stitches onto long pointed needles. 'He will take care of her and his mother will reward him. Oh, yes,' she continued, as though he'd spoken, 'Evelyn has bequeathed him most of her estate, and Jeremy also, is to receive a generous legacy. I understand that he intends to extend the married quarters.'

'And you?' he said, after a moment. 'Has she left *you* a legacy?'

She stiffened. 'I have sufficient funds for my requirements, Mr Winterbourne.'

And she began to knit very fast, the corner of her mouth twitching uncontrollably.

George stood up. He'd no wish to prolong the conversation. Now he understood why she had probably taken that late evening walk and the reason she'd not wanted him to alert Evelyn. Confident that her love was returned, Miss Darling had been devastated to learn that the will had been altered in Tim's favour. Well, he thought ruefully, making his way to the foot of the stairs, he and Miss Darling shared one thing in common: they'd both been rejected, and by the same woman.

When he reached his bedroom, he was surprised to see arranged in a crystal vase on his bedside table, a fine bunch of gold and red chrysanthemums. They were from Trina with a note saying she'd promised the flowers weeks ago and was sorry she'd taken so long. He puzzled over this for several minutes unable to recall any such conversation. Trina, of all people to give him flowers!

He wandered to the window and looked out. The snow was melting fast now, slopping heavy from branch to earth. It would be spring soon: the lawn a mass of daffodils, the Forsythia blazing, and the sweet smell of hyacinths filling the borders. He might have a go at pruning the shrub roses this year. Yes, cut away the weak and damaged stems. And there was plenty to be getting on with in the potting shed. He'd take a look in there tomorrow. Jeremy liked him to service the lawn mower and sharpen the tools; said he was better fitted for the job than Phil their old gardener. And perhaps he'd ask Jeremy if Alfred might be given some jobs around the place: he seemed at a bit of a loose end these days, did Alfred. It would do him good, get him out of himself. Yes, there was always plenty to take your mind off things.

THE GOLDEN SNAPDRAGON

'Don't be fribble Sybil. Choose something with less neck.'

'Surely more neck is acceptable for cocktail parties?' I reasoned.

But Great Aunt Beryl was having none of it. I turned the dress around. The neck was low yes, but might it, at a pinch, look more acceptable worn back to front? High back low front could translate as high front, low back. Such a divine style too. And it was a *Pierre Balmain*. Frivolous? Maybe just a little. I sighed and returned the pink rayon damask to its hanger. Perhaps Aunt was right, and she was paying after all.

'We could try *Swan and Edgar's*, Sibyl. And you can get a nice tea there. Come on, my treat.'

'You don't have to buy me tea Aunt, just because you were rude about the dress.'

'I know, but I want to and it's Christmas and you're my favourite niece. So quick march!'

'Did I ever tell you about your grandmother's friend Mufty and the dress she wore for a hunt ball?' The waitress laid out the tea and Aunt began pouring.

'No, Aunt,' I said, 'When was that?'

'A few years after the Great War. *You* eat my teacake, Sybil, I don't want it and by the time you've finished, I'll have finished my story.'

My hand reached for the plate. 'Well, if you're sure.'

She lit a cigarette. 'You won't remember Mufty. She was a friend of your grandmother; more of a dancing pal really: Low class dances they called them then. They'd roll up the drawing room carpets, play records and carry on like mad things dancing The Grizzly Bear, The Turkey Trot and all that caper. Her husband, Henry and your grandfather hated dancing, so why not? But on this particular night at this particular ball it seems that dancing was the last thing on Mufty's mind.'

'Sounds ominous. Go on.' I helped myself to more milk.

'The dance was held at Lord Penbury's estate - Penny we called him - and a private dinner preceded it. Your grandparents and I were invited along with Mufty and Henry. The place was decorated with streamers and there were photographs of the hunt pinned up for everyone to gawp at. And masks and brushes hung on the walls.'

'Foxes tails? How disgusting!'

'Don't interrupt Sybil! Guests were received by the master; and special guests, masters of the other hunt clubs and so on, were placed at the top table. The ballroom was awash with green foliage and japonica. It all looked very pretty and Mufty prettier than most in blue silk charmeuse. I remember being intrigued because she'd told me that four weights had been sewn into the hem of her train to keep it from flipping. She always spent a fortune on her gowns and looked stunning. Heads turned every time. Mufty was only little but had such a presence about her that one always thought of her as tall, do you know what I mean? And she always wore a spray of flowers. That year it was golden Antirrhinums beautifying those smiling lips and beguiling eyes.'

'Antirrhinums? What are they?'

'Snapdragons to you, darling. Henry was as sullen as ever, probably at the prospect of having to dance with some of the ladies. Anyway, he cheered up a bit when the chaps began singing hunting songs. And then Mufty took off.'

'You mean she disappeared'

'Precisely. At first we all thought she and your grandmother had gone to powder their noses, but when she failed to return, Henry grew disgruntled and drank too much.'

'But granny came back didn't she?'

'Yes. Your grandmother hadn't seen her either. Eyebrows were raised.

Aunt Beryl stubbed out her cigarette and fixed me with her mischievous blue eyes.

'Mufty was in love.'

'Ah! A secret assignation. Was he married?'

'It was far more complicated than that, dear.'

'Who was he Aunt?'

She squeezed my hand. 'You darling child! There are different kinds of love, you know.'

'I'm not a child,' I bristled. 'I'm fifty-five.'

'Well, you eat with a child's appetite. I see you've already finished the teacake. Have a scone.'

'No thank you Aunt.' I was miffed but I eyed them nonetheless.

'Henry wasn't interested in sex. Mufty had lovers, that was common knowledge. And her playing away relieved him of his marital duties.

Predictable behaviour on her part, I'd say. It was her unpredictable behaviour that made us all sit up that night. And it all began with her disappearance.'

'But she turned up eventually?'

'Oh yes. She turned up all right. You know, I don't mind if people do something a little crazy from time to time. Life would be too pedestrian for words if we didn't step out of line once in a while. But what I truly admire is originality. And Mufty was original, I'll give her that.'

'Did she confide in granny, do you think?'

'I doubt it. Your grandmother was too sweet, too innocent and bland to take on board anything in the least bit suspect. We all keep secrets from each other: the young from their parents, parents from their young. It makes no odds.'

I finally succumbed and reached for the scone. 'So if it wasn't a man she was in love with, what was it?'

'Money. She was in love with money. Men were just a game to her.'

'But surely Henry provided his wife with a generous allowance.'

'Henry was generous to a fault and that was their undoing. Mufty loved clothes but she loved gambling more and was heavily into debt. She daren't tell him. The shame of it, you see. But she knew that Penny had many gold sovereigns slashed away. And that night at the ball, she went to find 'em. She'd had a short affair with Penny while his wife, Felicity, was skiing in San Moritz so knew quite a bit about the man, his habits, even his savings and where he kept them it seems.'

'Did Lord Penbury know of the gambling debt?'

'No, and if she'd asked him for help, he'd have refused. They'd had a terrible row and broken up after he'd discovered her in bed with another man. Penny invited her to the ball for appearance's sake only.'

Aunt reached for her cigarettes. 'Do you smoke these days, Sybil?'

'You know I don't Aunt. I stopped after working in that smelly munitions factory.'

'Of course you did. Making aircraft blades, wasn't it? Brave girl. Who can believe we've survived two wars?'

'Do go on Aunt.'

'Well, Mufty left the party, sneaked up the back stairs, and made straight for Penny's bedroom. She knew the exact floorboard to go for. No flies on her. Using her metal comb she managed to lift it. And there they were: masses of shiny gold coins in an old chocolate box. She grabbed a handful, returned the floorboard and left. Now then, where was she to hide them?'

'In her evening bag?'

'Too risky. But what Mufty had brought in her evening bag were scissors, needle and thread. It later transpired that she hurriedly made for the nearest bathroom, locked the door, removed her train, unpicked the hem and taking out the little weights replaced them with the sovereigns. She then quickly stitched the hem back in place, popped the weights into her bag, unlocked the bathroom door and started to make her way downstairs. And that's when it all went wrong.'

'Why? What happened?'

'She descended via the main staircase this time. But as she was running down she came face to face with Penny's wife, running up. Who knows why Mufty suddenly tripped? Guilty feelings perhaps? Anyway, she lost her footing, screamed and careered down the remaining few steps.'

'Do you think Felicity pushed her?'

'Hardly. It was an accident and one which proved disastrous for the poor girl. There was a nasty splinter on the parkay floor and as she was being helped to a chair, her train caught on this splinter and tore the hem wide open. The sovereigns spilled out and rolled across the hall floor: under the chairs, beneath the ladies' ball gowns. Everywhere. It was quite awful. I saw the whole thing. Guests gasped. The game was up.'

'What happened to Mufty?'

'Henry forgave her of course, and paid her debts, but she was ruined socially. Nobody wanted to know the couple after that.'

'Did Lord Penbury press charges?'

'No. You know what our class is like: we close ranks, remain oyster. But there are plenty of cobwebs hanging around, believe me. I could tell you a dozen stories that would make your hair curl. But there's no time for that now. We've a dress to buy.'

'Well, Aunt, I tell you one thing,' I said, drawing back my chair, 'I won't be buying one with a train, that's for sure.'

MISS HENRY

Into the classroom she swept, bringing with her the warm smell of sandalwood and a rustle of petticoats. She removed her glasses, placed them next to the ink-well on her desk and surveyed her pupils.

'Good afternoon, girls.' Her clear voice rang to the back of the class.

A clatter of chairs replaced the chatter of fourth formers, as we rose to our feet and saluted our English teacher.

'Good afternoon, Miss Henry.'

'Be seated.'

We sat, looked into her young, unlined face and waited.

'What's the weather like out?'

On hot summer days she would sometimes ask this, as though having removed her spectacles, she was prevented from seeing for herself.

'Oh, please Miss Henry, can we?' came a voice from the back.

'Quiet, Sally Price! Do not beseech. It is vulgar.' And then turning to Brenda Blewitt, best at Latin and stealing other people's rubbers, 'You tell me, Brenda?'

'The sun is out, Miss Henry. It's very hot. Hot enough to …' She stopped, bit her lip and as the pause lengthened, we held our breath, waiting for the outcome.

'Very well girls,' Miss Henry said at last, apparently impressed by our lady-like constraint, 'As it is sunny and hot, we shall retire to the garden for our English lesson.'

A unified sigh: we were to be let out! Distanced from the reek of damp gabardine, ink impregnated desks and rotting floorboards. Sally Price, her gingham dress hitched up at the front with socks at half-mast, stifled exaggerated giggles as we made our way through the brown distempered passages that led to the garden. Our destination? The massive Cedar of Lebanon under whose dusky branches we placed our navy blue jumpers and sat. We didn't take books with us. Miss Henry's rich, expressive voice was the spoken word and leaning with her back to the trunk of the tree, she regaled in her light expressive voice, tales from Somerset Maugham, H.E. Bates and Charles Dickens. Her red hair was lightly coiled low on the nape of her neck, strands coming astray and blowing this way and that in the breeze. Her summer dresses were made of poplin and rustling taffeta, pulled in sharply at the waist, her slimness accentuated by thick elastic belts that mapped a well-defined figure.

My daydreams were plentiful as I gazed enviously into her alive face, with its dainty sprinkling of freckles. How old was she? Where did she live and was it alone? Did she have a secret lover? Happy to reveal fiction, Miss Henry kept facts about herself tightly under wraps. That was her glamour, her mystique: we knew so little about her - unlike our French teacher, Madame Dupois. Recently divorced, she spent our French lessons venting her fury. We learnt the language remarkably quickly on the strength of some of the lurid tales she regaled about her errant ex-husband.

Order marks were issued for misdemeanours committed by pupils attending Elmsfield Independent Grammar School for Girls.

'An order mark, Mary Jane, for daring to answer back.' Or, 'An order mark, Helen Ritchie, for not wearing your hat.' Or, 'That's an order mark, Lucy Parker,' fired at the vicar's daughter, who, instead of using the back stairs, which smelt of cabbage from the kitchens next door, took short cuts via the main staircase meant exclusively for staff and privileged sixth formers. Five order marks spelt a weekly detention, seven order marks, a Saturday morning detention. Staff took turns with the week-day detentions; Miss Long, our headmistress, always undertook the Saturday morning ones. Miss Henry, a relative newcomer to the school, eventually took her turn with the rest.

I attended her first detention duty. My sin was running instead of walking down a corridor. Late for a class, I had turned breathless into the hall, only to find my nose suddenly rammed against Miss Long's flat, chenille bloused bosom. She was grasping a can of air freshner, her index finger resolutely poised on the nozzle, feverishly intent on disinfecting the offensive smells produced by one hundred and fifty girls. Overactive sweat glands, scrunched aertex vests and unwashed hockey socks festering in shoe bags that lined darkened recesses under the stairs, evoked, 'Those vile odours!' as she put it. That we could not be responsible for the additional stench of damp and dry rot that permeated the dark, Victorian building was of no import and we suffered Miss Long's rigorous pollution on a twice weekly basis.

The usual punishments doled out at detentions were, learning by rote tedious speeches from Shakespeare and the age old writing out of lines comprising sentences such as, 'I must not talk in class,' or 'I must hand in my homework on time.' But Miss Henry's detentions were different. She didn't sit at the front of the class but amongst us, her long, silk-stockinged legs cramped behind one of the rickety desks. On first entering the room, I thought she'd not arrived and was gleefully planning my exit when a voice from the back of the classroom said:

'Are we all here? Just the six, is it?' With her glasses, sliding to the tip of her retrousse nose, she counted the five other heads and me. 'Good,' she said. 'Then we can begin.'

And then followed a very pleasant detention. Instead of issuing lines, or memorising passages, she asked each of us to write a short story. We were given a theme that particular week but we were usually allowed a free rein. Those less fortunate girls who did not have Miss Henry as an English teacher, were now blessed with her encouraging presence. Sitting by their side, she engaged their imagination with fragments of life either rooted in her past, or made up we were never sure, because she never said. But by writing our stories, by translating our dreams onto paper, she enabled us to explore our inner worlds. Her detentions now become an option, and one that many of us chose to take. It appeared no accident that the times Miss Henry was on duty, the order mark list was at its highest!

We looked forward to our annual summer dance. Beatles' numbers burst forth from record players as our stiff petticoats, pale pink and blue net confections flounced with pride, and our satin pointed-toed shoes felt the beat. We all brought food: sausage rolls, egg sandwiches, sausages, bags of crisps, pork pies, jellies and trifles; and as we swung the night away, the staff smiled benignly and drank over-diluted fruit punch. Spirits were strictly forbidden.

Madame Dupois was there, bangled and scented and gushing over a new man in her life, and so was Miss Henry but on her own, much to our disappointment. She disappeared every now and then but would pop up happy and smiling and even danced the twist with our curate, who came to the school once a week to teach Scripture.

It must have been around eleven o'clock when it happened. There were a number of us congregated in the hall, when suddenly Miss Long appeared standing motionless on top of the stairs. I think that I was the first to notice her: this tall, thin, shadowy figure wearing a long black crepe evening dress. She was holding something in front of her. At first, I couldn't make out what it was, but as she began her decent, slowly, deliberately, I saw that it was a bottle of whiskey. When she reached the bottom step, she stood and glared at us. Her lower lip trembled with rage. Her presence, her fury was palpable, and everyone went deathly quiet; only the strains of, *Love Me Do*, coming from the second form, contributed to any noise.

'I found this in the staff common room,' she boomed, brandishing the bottle like a sword. 'Spirits are strictly forbidden and the staff common room is out of bounds. There is a notice to that effect pinned on the door. This is a serious matter and I hope that whoever is responsible for this violation of school rules, will own up.'

There were some gasps; Sally Price tittered, the rest of us exchanged looks and as Miss Long turned and retraced her steps, I noticed the hem of her skirt beginning to unravel. A pity ... she must have given the performance of her life.

The summer holidays followed and when I returned in the September, now a fifth former, I was shocked and upset to learn that Miss Henry had left. The announcement was made at assembly by Miss Long who said that it was with regret that our English teacher had been obliged to resign on account of her sick mother who was too poorly be left on her own. She had been dismissed between a hymn, a prayer and the announcement of the new English teacher: a stern-faced woman with a disturbingly dark shadow over her upper lip.

The detentions decreased by five per cent, there was a general malaise among the upper school, the English marks plummeted and Madame Dupois announced her forthcoming second marriage.

It was during one of her French lessons that we learnt what may have happened. According to staffroom gossip, the bottle of whiskey found in Miss Long's study had belonged to Miss Henry, who had done the decent thing, owned up and handed in her notice.

'*Oui! Oui!*' Madame Dupois, her nicotine-voice reduced to a stage whisper, rolled heavily shadowed eyes 'She was a secret drinker. *Mon Dieu!* The strains of looking after 'er old mother, got to 'er, I think.'

We were sworn to secrecy, of course, and never found out if this were true or not but I did catch a glimpse of Miss Henry two years later. Whilst working in our local second hand bookshop, I came across two slim volumes of poetry by Elizabeth Jennings with Miss Henry's name inscribed inside the cover. The shop owner told me that my ex-English teacher was selling some of her books. She was planning to marry and live abroad - Italy, I think she said.

It was on my way home a week or so later that I caught sight of her walking arm in arm with the curate, the same curate who'd taught us Scripture and danced with her the night of the bottle incident. I didn't cross the road to speak to her, I don't know why, perhaps because I sensed their intimacy and didn't want to intrude. She was laughing like I'd never seen her laugh at school, without constrain, freely, spontaneously, as though she'd not a care in the world. If the story about her drinking had been true, then her life appeared to have taken a turn for the better.

School memories can change with the years: some become embellished, some fade while others are lost forever. School reunions bear this out: 'Do you remember that time when so and so happened?' can either be greeted with a positive whoop of recognition, or blank bewilderment. Different experiences mean different things to different people.

Miss Henry was a teacher among teachers and the memory *I* will always hold in *my* mind, is of seeing her that day so obviously happy and so completely in love, as she embarked on the rest of her life.

INCIDENT AT A BUS-STOP

Bowlby fainted.

He had rushed that morning, unwise with a dicky heart, snatched a cup of coffee and wasted time hunting for his bus-pass. When he finally reached the stop, his head was swimming and he felt nauseous - often a prelude to one of his 'turns'.

Trembling, he felt himself sway - the sky press down on his head, thunder roar in his ears and a desire to throw up.

When he came to, a woman wearing a balaclava was bending over him and peering into his face.

'I haven't any money!' Bowlby croaked, his heart in his mouth. 'But you can have my watch. It's in full working order, and worth a few bob.'

She took him firmly under the shoulders and pulled him to his feet.

'Get off!' cried Bowlby, giving her a shove. And then, 'Did you knock me out?'

'Knock you out? You passed out, you silly man!'

'Did I? Did I really? Oh yes! I expect I did. I'm sorry. I wasn't sure, you see. Your head gear ... A bit of a shock.'

And when she offered to call an ambulance:

'No! Thank you. I recover quite fast. This has occurred before.'

She grunted and turned away. But having said thus much, Bowlby felt compelled to elaborate.

'I suffer from low blood pressure, and my heart could be in better nick - nothing too serious. But I stupidly rushed before coming out. No proper breakfast. Not a good idea in my condition.'

Balaclava stood silent, her eyes fixed on the horizon.

'You can understand though, surely,' Bowlby continued, hanging onto the bus-stop for support, 'You can understand my having mistaken you for a ehm ... eh ...'

'A mugger? Out to get your pension book?'

'Well, to put it bluntly, yes. You must agree - that thing on your head is rather ...'

'My grandson wears it when skiing. It keeps out the wind.'

'Is he a crook too?' Bowlby quipped, risking a laugh.

'He's with The Prudential.'

'Well, that's all right then.'

No humour there.

Bowlby took several deep breaths and debated whether or not to sit down in the bus shelter. But if he sat and she stood, it might place him at a disadvantage. You could never be too sure with anyone these days. How long had she been there? He was sure he would have remembered seeing her, would probably, under the circumstances, have walked on to the next stop. If she hadn't been wearing vivid blue eye shadow, he would have thought her a fellow in that get-up: leather trousers, a worn flying jacket and that ghastly thing on her head.

He tried to take his mind off things by admiring his new lambs-wool lined overcoat bought from a reputable catalogue.

'I rather hoped this might be a 201,' he said, as he watched a green double-decker sail past. 'Are you waiting for the 201?'

'The 205.'

'That's even slower - the 205.'

'Hence the balaclava.'

Touché!

Bowlby felt in his pocket for one of his pills.

'Bus services are not what they were,' he said, popping one under his tongue. 'I've waited as long as half an hour for a 201.'

She nodded and sat down, her legs splayed out in front of her - Long legs. Not a bad shape, Bowlby thought, deciding it now safe to follow suit.

He supposed that he should have realized from the onset that she was only trying to help, but when you were ill things took on a new look, a new dimension. How could he have known the woman wasn't after his money? She had helped him, and he was grateful, but there was no cause for her to be so stand-offish. He had apologized, after all. Bowlby hated atmospheres; and he hated to be overlooked - passed over.

'Learn to fight your own battles.' Bowlby could still hear his mother's voice. Would it ever fade? That critical castigating tone she had used on him more often than not.

'Stand up for yourself. Don't be such a cry baby! Hit him back. Wallop him hard!' when Bowlby came home bleeding and blubbing after Bayliss from the upper fourth had set on him. And what support had he ever had when his brother cajoled him into handing over his pocket money so that he could take his blasted girl friend to the flicks?

It didn't matter what he'd done, or how hard he'd tried, nothing seemed to have pleased his mother. Of course she had always favoured Bernard: a scholarship to grammar school, a place at Cambridge. It had done Bowlby no favours either, his bearing so strong a resemblance to his father who had left them all in the lurch. He must have been a constant reminder to his mother of the man she came to hate.

A bit of attention, a bit of affection, of praise that was all he had asked. But then what had he done for his mother to be proud of? - A clerk to a firm of solicitors. Did that merit praise? Why, he hadn't even managed to get himself hitched: Nearly but not quite. His mouth felt dry, a second wave of nausea hit him and he held onto the sides of the bench to steady himself.

Janet had made a fool of him all right - a laughing stock - walking out on him two weeks before the wedding. Another man, so she had said. He was no great catch, he knew that, but he was reliable, considerate and had tried to be loving - not easy when you'd received none. But he knew how to show kindness and consideration towards the girl: had laid down a decent deposit on a nice flat in a good area, seen to all the wedding arrangements. The whole episode had been unfair, unjust. Unkind. People could be so unkind.

Balaclava was unkind - unbending, unforgiving. He had said he was sorry. He had shown gratitude, tried to be friendly but she wasn't having any. Well, he'd jolly well make Balaclava notice him. He'd make her unbend. So he would! He'd tried making her laugh, that hadn't worked, so he'd make her jump instead: Anything to remove that implacable expression from those dark, cold eyes.

There was a drain a few yards from his feet and as he stared into its brown murky water, a faint smile began to play on his lips. He opened his mouth, and almost before he knew it yelled:

'A rat! Look!'

Balaclava slowly switched her gaze from the horizon to where he was pointing a long shaky finger.

'I don't see a rat.'

'Down there by the gutter: A big, brown furry rat with a long tail. It must have climbed through the grid.'

'I used to keep a rat,' Balaclava now calmly returning to her former eye-line.

Damn and blast the woman! fumed Bowlby and began picking at his cuticles.

A few moments later Balaclava opened a large black leather bag, drew out a small coffee flask, pulled down the mouth piece of her head gear and drank. To his utter surprise, she turned and offered the flask to him.

He felt himself brighten. Maybe it had worked. Maybe that jolt had woken her up a bit, done her the power of good.

He took the flask, thanked her, placed it to his lips and pretended to drink. A hot drink was just what he needed right now, but if the woman had kept a rat, maybe more than one, there was no knowing what health hazards lurked within her walls, or her drinking vessels.

He pretended to drink, returned the flask; felt inspired then to ask if she lived locally.

'No,' she said, packing it away.

'Been to visit a friend perhaps?'

'No.'

My God! She must have made some man a frigid wife. But why should he care? She didn't matter a jot to him. He'd never see her again. If she didn't want to talk that was her affair. And yet it was her detached coolness, her imperturbability that drew Bowlby inexplicably towards her.

A large puddle stood markedly between them. For some moments he sat staring into its murky centre. Slowly he got to his feet, pretended to steady himself and then with a sudden cry stumbled into the pool. A spray of black water rose high into the air.

'Oh, I'm so sorry!' he cried. 'I must have lost my balance. Are you soaked?'

'Afraid not. Hard luck!'

'My knees give way sometimes,' he defended, not looking at her. 'Knee mice, you know.'

'You seem to possess an affinity with rodents.'

He glared at his wet trouser bottoms. His face burned with a child's humiliation. How dare she mock him!

'I still have excellent reflexes, you see,' she continued. 'During the war, I was an S.O.E. agent. I'm used to all sorts of mayhem.'

Bowlby opened his mouth to speak, but no sound came. An S.O.E. agent! Balaclava engaged in espionage, sabotage, and reconnaissance?

Of course! Why that would explain everything. Her silence, her reticence, her manly appearance and last but not least, that black thing covering her head and half her face.

A taxi approached and slowed down in the hope of a fare.

'We could share, if you like,' he blustered.

'I haven't money for taxis,' she said.

Should he offer to help? He had been childish there was no getting away from it. No wonder she had been so reticent - how difficult it must be to change one's ways, one's attitudes even after all these years. Prudency, caution must have become second nature to her.

The taxi picked up speed and disappeared into the distance.

'I shall walk,' Balaclava suddenly announced.

'I'm sure the bus won't be much longer,' said Bowlby. He wanted her to know there was no hard feeling. That he understood.

'I can't wait any longer. I have an appointment,' she said.

A sudden wave of panic engulfed him. She was leaving. Going. He would never set eyes on her again. He would never be able to surprise her and she would never bend to his will, or remember him with anything other than contempt. Most of all, he wanted to say sorry but didn't know how.

A lump rose in his throat and tears threatened his eyes: the tears of a lonely school boy; the tears of a young man rejected in love and the tears of an old man whose life had been soured by his own reactions to it.

'I may as well walk with you,' he said in a last ditch attempt.

Balaclava hesitated. And for one brief moment he thought her eyes relaxed, softened.

'I prefer to walk alone. But thank you,' she said.

'Then I shall have to wait for my bus,' Bowlby replied, more sturdily than he felt. 'Thank you again for your help.'

She extended her hand, and he noticed, as he shook it, how curiously small it was.

After an abrupt nod of farewell, Balaclava strode off in the direction of the nearby town. Her step was sure, firm and Bowlby watched her grow dim with distance; this large, ungainly woman with the small hands.

She was about to turn the corner, when the bus came. It was the 205. Her bus. He opened his mouth to call her. But already she had gone.

THE VISIT

'You are part of my life,' she says, hugging me, kissing me and shimmering with sorcery. She is through the front door, down the hall and into the kitchen before you can say, Merry Christmas! Small damp footprints treading cream carpet: The house already hers.

Hot travelled, her swollen shoulder bag spills half-used packets of aspirin and scrunched up tissues onto the floor. She sinks into the nearest chair, wipes a botoxed forehead with the back of her hand and asks what's new?

'Not a lot,' I say, affecting the casual air reserved for old friends. And I make us gins and tonic, swallowing mine quickly, hungry to relax. A sliver of ice slips down my throat and I gasp.

'I wish you'd 'phoned, Isabel. Wish you'd told me you were coming.'

I still have to buy cards, put up the tree and make a batch of mince pies.

'Well, you know me, impetuous as ever,' she says, whilst foraging in her bag for cigarettes. 'I was in the area and simply couldn't go home without calling. It's been such ages. And it is Christmas,' she adds, looking up with a dimpled smile.

I nod, but feel vaguely discomforted by her presence: am more accustomed to her letters now; hastily scrawled words trailing expensive, cream notepaper. Nowadays, our friendship is better served by absence; those dividing years that severed our girlhood bonds changing the format with the times: fashion, rock groups, the pill and that final disjunction, marriage.

'It's as though we'd never been apart,' she says, her voice husky with smoke and contrivance, and leaning towards me takes my hand and places her bets. 'Could you put me up - just for a few nights?'

Those green eyes shift and I startle at their slyness. Is this the tenor of survival: the currying of friendships, fighting for rights, for self-esteem?

'I've had an offer on my house,' she says, agitating her string of pearls. 'I want to look at properties. This area might suit me very well.'

'You didn't write you were moving,' I blurt. 'What about your cottage - that beautiful cottage? It's yours now.'

She lifts narrow shoulders, exposing a chest grown bony with age.

'Well, Beth, I'm bored. Too much time on my hands, that's the truth of it. And it might be rather fun to move. Give me something to do, pretty up a new house. So I thought Bournemouth. I'll move to Bournemouth. The air's so good round here, so clement; and now that my divorce is finally settled, it might help me to forget: A new life, new beginnings and all that.'

Another smile: a slow conspiratorial parting of the lips.

'He wants me back, you know. Once the mistress leaves they can't cope. Oh, yes. A man needs a woman. Well, he can whistle for me because I intend to spend his money, every last penny of it. Life could be fun, don't you think, Beth? Living so close. Be like old times.'

I get to my feet to mix us more drinks and in my haste, trip over her bag; feel her eyes heavy lidded, moist, watching me, mocking me, as I slice the lemon and pour the tonics.

'I wouldn't stay for long, Beth, just a few days.'

You said that last time I want to shout, dropping large ice cubes into tall glasses. The time you walked out on Harry and turned up on our doorstep in floods of tears. One night, you said, and stayed three months: burnt a hole in our sofa, borrowed a brooch you never returned, used all the hot water and smoked the air black. But the rules of friendship do not permit this. A friend in need …

'Have you a spare night dress?' she whispers, my silence taken as consent.

A shaky smile awaits my approval and I give it but only, I warn, for one night. After that, oh dear! I'm not sure. John might be coming home early, may have made plans. If only John were here. But John is not here; he is away in Texas, on business. I must make my own decisions, settle my own scores. But how to tell your ex flat-mate, bridesmaid, once confidante that she is not welcome, not wanted? And I can hear John's voice, adamant, firm: 'One night only. No more, Beth. Please.' The undoing of all those pen-filled years?

'Let me know in the morning, Beth,' Isabel says later, whilst breezily scanning the prettily chintz-patterned spare bedroom. 'I can always find a hotel. I would hate to put you out.' There is the familiar edge to her voice, that underlying admonishment I remember so well.

After a late supper, following an evening of strained reminiscences not helped by our ageing memories, we say good night. It seems that those intermittent meetings: theatre outings, concerts, lunch at the Savoy Grill, were buttressed by our surroundings; provided talking points that helped fill those gaping years: But here, in this house, surrounded by my solitude, we are strangers, our fellowship outmoded, spent.

Now, as I lay in bed, listening to her pad back and forth to the bathroom, I wonder about her moving house. Is it to be nearer to John and me? Could it be that she is lonely? Oh God! I can see her now, taking over our kitchen with her loud chat, coarse laugh, jokes and ribaldry that I once found so joyous: Perhaps not. The years have taken their toll on us both and maybe she has played the injured wife too well and for too long. Her features, once strong and impressive have slackened, drooped, grown pettish with want of control. There is no cosmetic treatment for disaffection and a restless soul.

I pull the covers close, toss and turn, disquietude wrestling with reason. How can I desert her? Desert? Too strong a word, surely. Isabel is independent and as stubborn as ever and now, thanks to Harry's generosity, a rich woman. Strange, how after all these years, the memory of her glamour still touches me. I still look forward to her letters, even to those untrimmed, angry outpourings surrounding Harry and his mistresses. Her wit: salty, abrasive still pockets moments of hilarity, evanescing to a time that was festive for us both.

As a student, new to London from my sleepy country town, the ebullient, adventurous Isabel, popular and loud, took me under her wing; chose me, the quiet unassuming girl from the provinces, as her friend and confidante. Such privilege, as I deemed it, demanded a certain compliance on my part but I was amenable, meek by nature and the rewards meant automatic entry into her circle: the so called elite who inspired envy and praise from the less intrepid, less impetuous students of our year. As I followed in her trail, I longed to be like her, cherished even her darker sides: her tantrums and vagaries, ignorant of the dangers of such an enchantment.

I wake to my decision. Whilst showering, dressing, listening to Isabel's smoky cough as she bangs in and out of the bathroom, I remain firm, intent; knowing with sad certainty that this latest meeting can only end as it had begun, in politeness.

Greeting Isabel on the landing, I tell her that I am sorry but she cannot stay longer. I offer no excuses. Preparing to go downstairs, we face each other and our pasts: our salad days, our lustrous youth.

She inclines her head, regal in rejection, her shoulders tight and drawn as she brushes past me. Our fortitudes, for these they are, have found us out and now we must confront them.

We breakfast in silence - cups against saucers, knives against plates. Isabel crumbles her toast, slips slivers between petulant lips; sips coffee, her painted mouth lingering against the rim of her cup. I clear my throat, she coughs; I offer more coffee, she declines. And not one word passes between us.

Later, with hands rope-veined and slightly trembling, she lays her napkin on her plate whilst I roll and place mine in its silver ring: stretching the moment, fearing our next moves.

Slowly Isabel rises to her feet, stretches her back and gazes out of the window: at the beeches leaning into the wind and the postman walking up the garden path. She asks if she might use the telephone directory and when I meet her gaze that vacant hurt I dreaded is not there. Instead, her eyes are shining, bold and clear.

Fetching the directory from under the stairs, I hand it to her and watch as she thumbs the pages, her face flushed and fresh with excitement. At length her red nailed fingertip rests under the name, Alistair Baldwin. A friend, an old flame, is he? There had never been a shortage of men in her life. The beautiful, provocative Isabel, sartorially resplendent, disciplined in the art of body maintenance and culinary abstinence. Wafer thin when the rest of us were puppy fat, she dedicated her life to dieting and did rather well out of it: expensive gifts, copious lovers and a nugatory life style rich with all the social perks.

'Who is he?' I ask. 'This Alistair Baldwin?'

'An old friend,' she replies, her mouth tight with secrets.

'The telephone's in the hall,' I say, as she scribbles the man's address onto a scrap of paper.

'Oh, I don't think I'll 'phone,' says she, her lips quivering delight. 'I'd rather turn up. Surprise him.' Of course.

Newly charged, she runs upstairs to bathe and dress before pressing yesterday's outfit, an expensive two piece cotton suit.

We set off soon after that, driving the four or so miles to where he lives.

She asks me to drop her off at the corner of his road: a paint-glossed crescent of town houses interlocked with affluence. I switch off the engine to say our good byes and she turns to face me, thanks me for having her: at once polite and convivial while her vivid eyes agitate to be off.

'What if he's out?' I ask, anxiety surfacing. 'What will you do if your friend's not there?'

She lifts eyebrows, haughty and thin. Men have always been there for her, why should now be different?

We kiss our farewells. There are no promises to meet again, or to keep in touch and after opening the car door and lowering long, silk-stockinged legs onto the pavement, she slams it shut and fast steps towards her quarry. Not once does she look back.

I am glad to get home and immediately go into the kitchen to make coffee, black and strong. It is good to have the house to myself again. But the air is heavy. Isabel is everywhere. Her heady scent tracks me from room to room: the hall, the study, the sitting room.

I open the windows. The wind has dropped and now the winter sun, milky with haze, warms my face as I listen to the distant traffic and the children at the nearby school, practising for their Christmas concert.

Slowly I make my way upstairs and into the guestroom. It holds that familiar emptiness of one who has just left. The normally untidy Isabel, has folded the sheets and blankets and placed them at the foot of the bed. The silver brush and comb set are neatly arranged on the dressing table and the chair's cushions plumped and positioned exactly as I had left them.

Only as I turn to go, do I notice her belt: a black, wide, shiny, patent leather belt with a bold brass buckle, lying forgotten on the bedside table.

And I feel the loss: Isabel gone.

5 GRESHAM PLACE

Our stately home has closed; shut down by force of circumstance. Only now can I tell my story. Now that the case is over, punishments meted and the crowds dispersed.

I write this because I want to tell the facts as they were: obviate those preconceived ideas fed so insidiously to you, the readers of our national press. And although I am powerless to change events, I can at least attempt to put the records straight even perhaps, change your opinion of us: we, once the inhabitants of 5 Gresham Place.

Let me jog your memory: Jeremy. Remember him? Of course you do. Everyone remembers Jeremy. The painter who faked *Roses on a Grand Piano* by the late Xavier Benoit. My husband Jeremy, charged, sentenced, lifted from the art elite and relocated to Wormwood Scrubs. Don't ask me why he did it. I am moneyed. He is talented. But Jeremy liked living on the edge and perhaps that is why he did it. Perhaps he was bored after many years of married life. Or there again, perhaps he determined to prove his financial independence. Who knows? We never scratched very much below the surface, he and I.

Art was his life. He painted, mounted exhibitions and ran up huge bills. When he couldn't pay, I did.

His prison sentence was reduced owing to good behaviour and on his release and through a contact, managed to get a part-time job at a polytechnic teaching eighteenth century art and crafts to mature students.

The tabloids pestered him for his story and his vanity complied. The proceeds paid off his overdraft while his teaching job demonstrated his humility and a way back into the hearts of the public domain. And so it was there, midst the paintbrushes, oils, the turpentine and the temperaments that he had his 'brainchild', as he termed it. We would, he announced, his love of things precarious rising to the surface, restore our Georgian house to its former glory and open it to the public.

Gresham Place, my girlhood home is what I am talking about: a place so familiar to me that I barely noticed its physical attributes. At fourteen

I had been placed in the reluctant care of my aunt, my mother's sister, while my parents whisked themselves off to India and a colourful, colonial life that cut theirs short, rendering me an orphan by the age of nineteen. Parental guidance took the form of once monthly cheques and two page letters written on fine linen notepaper which issued directives as to my physical and moral welfare.

Although my time spent with Aunt Bea was during the nineteen fifties, I conformed to a Victorian-type life style. My schooling, convent based, brought its own restrictions. Few friends were encouraged to call and my duty was first and foremost to my aunt, an irritable and impatient spinster who complied with her sister's wishes, which sprung rather more from a sense of duty rather than any affection for me. She was never well and took to her bed on numerous occasions. When it was finally discovered that she had terminal cancer, a nurse was engaged and she remained with my aunt to the end.

I first met Jeremy when he came to Gresham Place to look at some paintings Aunt Bea wanted to sell. She possessed several fine oils left to her by a rich relative. When she died, she left me the house, an unexpected legacy, I have to say.

I always maintained that Jeremy fell in love with the house and married me. I suppose that I was an ideal foil for him and I came to my marriage tame with my natural sense of duty well and truly entrenched.

Nestling in the Chilterns, Gresham House was to be our one and only marital home. Large, elegant and formal, the three storey house had been in Aunt Bea's family since the reign of George the second. The frontage led up to a large panelled front door above which was a semi-circular fan glass window affording light to a good sized hall that was hung with tapestries and a number of ancestral paintings. There were many rooms including a well-equipped library. Oh yes, it was a handsome property in need of a makeover. My parents had left me a generous annuity that would go some way to help pay for the renovations. The rest was up to us.

First, we set about repairing the exterior. The hipped roof needed re-tiling and its heavy wooden cornice replacing. New drains and window frames had to be installed. As work progressed, I became caught up in Jeremy's enthusiasm. Like all his projects, he worked tirelessly drumming up new commissions from his few remaining contacts while continuing to teach the while.

Eventually we were ready to begin work on the interior. The drawing room with its fine mouldings and ornamental motifs needed re-plastering before being papered. After painting the room a golden yellow, Jeremy bought a Georgian chandelier with curved arms, made from metal, wood and glass. It was beautiful and must have cost the earth. The walls were hung with legitimate copies of eighteenth century landscapes and these were formally grouped around a basket grate fireplace with a cast iron back and a front that was decorated with swags and urns. Most stuff he bought at auctions bidding for English designers like George Smith Sheraton and Manwaring.

The kitchen was a nightmare, because we had to tear out all the modern appliances and install, as near as possible, eighteenth century stuff. That took a bit of finding, I can tell you. We built an extra room onto the back and bought a microwave oven, moved the washing machine and fridge in there and covered the window with a gold, brocade curtain so that nobody could see in. On the door was a sign, 'Private. Staff Only'.

The dining room was a real feature, with candles in sconces on the dark green-embossed walls and draped swatches of material that we had picked up while on holiday in Venice. Upstairs, the bedrooms and bathroom were again copies of the period with four poster beds and abbreviated canopies.

We settled on an admission fee of £10.50 which included a guide booklet written by me and coffee, tea and scones. Delia did all that. I complained that she put too much bicarbonate of soda in the scones but she wouldn't listen: stubborn, like her brother. She had come to live with us just prior to Jeremy's conviction. I felt disquieted by the notion of having an extra person in our house. But I kept reminding myself how lucky I was to have found Jeremy. Had it not been for my aunt's patronage of the arts, I might never have met him. To have refused his sister refuge, a relative who had been left high and dry by a husband who had stolen her savings and run off to Thailand would have seemed heartless. Besides I was unused to asking for things, my values based not so much on moral principles but rather a simple lack of self-discovery.

I had begun to question my feelings towards Delia during Jeremy's sentence. Prison life had changed him - of course it must have done - He was restless, brooding and prone to moods. When I went to visit him he would ask for Delia.

'You haven't brought Delia,' he would say, sounding peeved.

It was the anxious frustration of a child parted from its mother. Maybe this had something to do with their being twins. Aren't they supposed to feel each other's pain, plug into each other's psyche? So, shrugging inwardly, I cut down on the visits and sent Delia instead. She was more than happy to take my place. But I detected in her a smugness as though she almost relished usurping my place.

After his release, Jeremy continued to turn to her for guidance. And how she thrived on it: almost following in his wake, seeing to his every need, accompanying him on trips to art shops and auctions. While wishing she would go and leave us on our own to re-discover our marriage and find our own way back together again, my inner anxiety, my innate desire to please, to be liked, remained paramount and I made every effort to ignore my nagging feelings of jealousy and resentment. I tried to include her in things - conversation, opinions and advice, but the more I tried the more she appeared to frown at my efforts. It seemed I could never win. The twins would not be separated and how could I be so wicked as to wish ill on a sixty-five year old woman with a wooden leg?

I was tidying the post card rack one evening when Jeremy, wearing his Wellington boots, stomped into the hall and demanded that I come outside.

I left my desk and followed him into the garden. It was July. Spring had slipped peacefully into summer and our opening few weeks had seen a heartening number of visitors. The bush roses were in bloom and the multi-flowered Floribundas and the Patio roses shed their delicate shell pink petals all across the lawn. Jeremy was standing puce faced next to the spiral topiary, brandishing Delia's walking stick with which he now parted a cluster of peonies and stabbed at a long pale condom.

'How on earth did that get there?' I gawped.

'That's what I'd like to know.'

'Perhaps the wind?' I offered, lamely.

'And these? You think the wind blew these in too?' now hooking a pair of cream, lace briefs onto the stick and waving them back and forth like a flag.

I felt my face burn and without another word, ran into the house, returning minutes later with gloves and a small polythene bag which I handed to him.

'This can mean only one thing,' he growled, using the stick as a shovel. 'Members of the visiting public have been at it.'

'Well, yes Jeremy, it does look as though ...'

'Behind our backs, they've been at it.'

'They'd hardly do it in front of us, would they, dear?'

'I will not tolerate it!'

Now he rooted among the Salvias and the Delphiniums. The Pinks were flattened, the Clematis jabbed and the Orange Blossom bush given a stern shaking.

'There's only one thing for it,' he said, straightening his long, thin back and looking at me with watery, grey eyes.

'Oh, no, Jeremy!' I shook my head in horror. 'Please, not that.'

'Punters!'

'Yes, dear, but ...'

'They must be watched.'

'But Jeremy, you know how I hate public speaking.'

'Only way to keep an eye on things, old girl. You wrote a good enough pamphlet, you can make a passable tourist guide.'

It was useless to argue; his mind, obdurate as ever, was made up; and so over the next few days I put pen to paper and prepared a talk about our house conversion. This I practised on Delia, who sat poker-faced throughout, her false leg stretched out in front of her as though waiting to be fitted for shoes.

Visitors liked to touch. They stroked the flock wallpaper, ran hands over dust bloomed tabletops and plucked the strings of our recently acquired harp. Following the breakage of a 1760 Derby basket, notices with the words: 'Please do not touch', were strategically placed in every room and in the garden. But still they fingered: lifted, rubbed and pinched the silk curtains, remarking on quality and value. They poked the oil paintings to check they were real and in the garden, children threw pebbles into the ornamental pool. I pointed meaningfully towards the notice nailed to the *Pride of India*, but was rewarded with blank looks of denial. Oh, well. Who owns up to anything these days? No matter how thorough your surveillance, there will always be someone who slips through the net. Like Petronella for instance.

She arrived on a late September afternoon; one of five visitors. Tall and wafer thin; a creature who might dedicate their life to dieting and do rather well out of it. Striking she was, tossing that long, auburn hair of hers and touching - touching everything with long, indolent fingers - not with disregard but rather as a dealer might - thoughtfully, a knowledgeable frown impressing her young, high brow. I gave my usual polite smile, pointed to the notice and was rewarded with an absent-minded nod whilst her slim fingers continued to caress.

That night, exhausted after a busy day, Jeremy and I retired earlier than usual. We walked along the long oak panelled landing, opened our bedroom door, switched on the light and there she was: the girl with the auburn hair, fast asleep on top of our bed. We stood with mouths open, staring. Long strands of hair like fronds, lay across her face as she breathed deeply and evenly.

Jeremy rounded on me. What was I playing at? Had I not checked that all visitors had gone? Had I forgotten the condom and knickers episode? There'd be sex in our bed next. Well, I thought. That would make a change.

The girl stirred, opened her eyes, sat up and swung shapely legs over the side of the bed.

'Where am I?' she asked, her voice creamy with sleep.

And then seeing the closed curtains and us bent over her, 'Is it late? How awful! I must have dropped off. I'm so, so sorry!'

'But I don't understand,' I spluttered. 'You were with my group. I remember seeing you. What happened?'

She lowered her head and lifted her eyes.

'I'm afraid I slipped back in here when you were showing everyone the other bedrooms. A bad habit of mine, dropping off in other people's houses. I can't resist comfortable beds. I have a low blood count, you see, and I tire easily. I sleep for hours on end.'

Now she was looking at Jeremy. 'I lie down just for a moment, and before I know it, I've nodded off. And your bed is so comfortable.'

Then turning to me, 'Might I have a glass of water?'

I glanced at Jeremy. His face had softened, his body relaxed.

'Go and ask Delia if she has any tea and scones left over, will you, Harriet?' he said now looking at her as though transfixed.

'Should I order a taxi?' I asked.

'That won't be necessary. She can stay here for tonight.'

Dressed in her *robe a la francaise* with its close fitting bodice that showed off her high white breasts, Petronella played, the 'lady of the house' to perfection. Gliding hither and thither, smiling at the visitors, reclining on window seats, her role was a decorative one intended to enhance the atmosphere of an eighteenth century house.

After receiving favourable comments from the visitors, Jeremy decided to dress up too and returning to the theatrical costumiers from where he had hired her dress, secured his own outfit, complete with a white, full bottom wig. Delia, after a good deal of persuasion on Jeremy's part and a good deal of muttering on hers, agreed to dress up as a servant. Oh, yes, it all worked very well. It seemed they had hit lucky finding Petronella, the ex-drama student from Surrey: so popular with the public, so talented. But for how long would she stay? Surely she would seek theatre work, or secure an agent for films and television? Living with us could hardly advance her career. But no, it seemed she was content to role-play, receiving her keep and a little pocket money in return.

I can see the two of them so clearly even now: in the drawing room, she sitting in the window-seat with her embroidery, Jeremy nearby in a winged-backed chair, quietly reading. Or outside, on the stone garden seat with their poetry books. Or, when Jeremy painted Petronella's portrait as she posed in her sack gown and lace ruff.

And the visitors loved it all.

'How charming,' they all said, glancing bashfully in their direction.

These new ventures, so well received, spelt success for Jeremy, who chuckled with a child's eagerness each time he donned his costume; his repletive smile bypassing me and resting instead on Petronella's unrestrained face.

Had I been included in this charade, perhaps I would have felt part, or at least pretended to feel part of this tight little group, but Jeremy insisted I wear my *Burberry* skirt, twin set and pearls: so tasteful, so English - a hint of class, you know. And so I did; my face masked with weary cheeriness.

As the weeks went by, Jeremy grew calmer, more reasonable enabling me to get on with my chores in relative peace. But the busier I became the more I seemed to disappear: the couple staking their places and lessening mine. Sometimes I caught Delia watching me: a small smile lifting her pain tight lips. She knew and I hated her for it. Her eternal forbearance towards her brother was as strong as ever.

It was late October and we had closed the doors on the last visitors of the season. Taking Petronella's hand, Jeremy led her into our kitchen where Delia and I were preparing dinner. He knew only too well that having the girl by his side sabotaged any resistance from me and while Delia sliced carrots into uniformed strips, and I set the dials on the microwave, he took from the fridge a bottle of champagne and popped the cork.

'Well, girls,' he declared, 'we've done it. Here's to our first successful season.' And the bubbles rose high in our glasses, spilling over onto the formica work top and Petronella let down her hair and shook it back and forth.

'Thank you,' she cried, 'Oh, thank you for taking me in.' And to Delia, 'Your wonderful scones! Will you teach me how to make them?'

But Delia turned her back, took up her knife and chopped harder, drowning the conversation that now ensued between Jeremy and Petronella. When they had finished, the two of them faced me, their bodies close, their heads touching and I knew then that she would never leave.

The second season saw a change in Delia. She became quieter, even more withdrawn and had taken to scowling at the visitors. Her scones once soft and warm were now cold and hard with the tea tepid and overly strong. Jeremy no longer needed Delia: her approval, her loyalty were all wasted on him. As for me, I went along with it all because despite everything, I still loved my husband. But Jeremy loved Petronella. That I could not change. He was an old man, years older than I, with little sexual energy left and so his infatuation for the girl remained within the bounds of decency. If he was better natured towards me, not necessarily nicer but easier, that was worth something, I reasoned. And like the old with the young, he indulged her. She with her lightening moods, her moue and sudden rages were all acceptable in his eyes. When she left candles burning, or neglected to say if she would be away for the night, or when she slammed doors causing cracks to form on the ceiling, her reputation remained intact. She was his celebration, his *raison d'etre;* her increasing demands dismissed, overlooked, excused: her merriment, light heartedness as he deemed it, meritorious of forgiveness.

Delia and I were different. We found her presence onerous, irksome: an incursion and a burden to be nursed daily. I learnt to honey my voice, mask my fear, my growing contempt. It was the chary despair of one who has lost.

And then along came Ira. Tall, angular and dark, his black hair falling about his eyes in fat, careless waves.

As I guided the visitors around the house, Jeremy and Petronella were seated on the garden bench, folders in their laps, waiting for us to join them so that they may begin their poetry recital. Oh, yes, they gave those now when the weather was fine.

I directed people towards the weather-proof chairs arranged in a small arc. Once they were settled, Petronella began reading a Shakespearean sonnet. Her voice was soft, caressing. She met this young man's gaze, held it; and afterwards, as she and Jeremy walked back to the house, Ira waylaid them. He told them he was also an actor and did they need anyone else to join the team? Of course they did, she replied at once and begged Jeremy to engage him.

With Ira now part of the group, Jeremy grew agitated and cross. His walk became slower, his gait more halting, and he complained of pains in his chest. He was painfully aware of their lovemaking, as locked in her bedroom at odd times of the day, neither attempted to smother cries of physical pleasure. The poetry recitals dwindled with Ira frequently away supposedly attending auditions, and Petronella, moody in his absence, and unsure of his devotion, flatly refused to take part without him. Instead, the visitors had to make do with my little tours and Delia's hard baked scones.

I begged Jeremy to send them both away but he flatly refused. So I did it instead - one evening after we had closed. Ira had taken a temporary job up north, and Jeremy had gone to an auction in London and would be home late.

'Why do you stay?' I asked Petronella, while stacking away the dinner plates. 'Surely you want more than this.'

'We like the set up.' Her voice was hard and flat.

'But Ira will leave before long,' I said, conscious of the shaky voice. 'He'll get work in the theatre or films - a good looking man like him.'

She laughed. 'You think so?'

'Of course.'

'Ira isn't an actor. Surely you must see that. The way he recites. He's hopeless.'

'But you said …' I stared incredulous.

'Ira's far too shrewd to be an actor.' She was brushing her hair now with long, even strokes. 'He's an astute business man though, I'll give him that. He sees an opportunity and moves in.'

'Like here, you mean?' I could hardly breathe.

She laid her brush aside and faced me.

'Ira and I want to buy your house.'

'I beg your pardon?'

'We would like to buy you out.'

'Does Jeremy know of this?'

'Yes.'

'But, but he's said nothing to me.'

'Perhaps he has his reasons.'

'Reasons? What reasons?'

'Oh, come on! You know as well as I do what he's been up to.'

'With you?'

'Not with me,' she sneered. 'What do I want with an old man like him?'

'What on earth are you talking about?'

'You think that it's all stopped don't you? That he completed his prison sentence and now he's being a good boy.'

'What are you implying, Petronella?'

'You're a bit of an ostrich, Harriet. How do you think he afforded that hideous tasteless chandelier?'

'He knows people in the trade. I don't ask questions.'

'No, I bet you don't.' And then changing track. 'My parents are rich, One day I will be too.'

'I've no doubt.' I remarked dryly.

'When Jeremy was painting my portrait, he told me things.'

'Things? What things?'

'That he passes on some of his paintings to a certain dealer who passes them off as originals.'

'You're lying!'

'Ask Jeremy,' she shrugged.

'Of course I won't ask Jeremy,' I shouted. 'I wouldn't insult him.'

Another shrug.

'And Ira?' I said trembling.

'Ira and I have known each other a long time. As a youngster he never had much incentive to work. I think he must have known he'd come into money one day. When I went on to study drama, he hung about waiting for his old man to die. But the old bugger refuses to turn his toes up. But when he does ...'

'Come outside!' I said, and my sudden change of tone must have taken her by surprise because she followed me un-protesting into the garden.

It was dusk. Through the kitchen window I could see the lace-cap hydrangeas with their faded lilac blooms drip water from a recent downpour. The last of the honey suckle and night stocks smelt rich and sweet in the wet. It was all so peaceful, so tranquil it was difficult to believe that this woman could sweep it all from under our feet.

'Do you know,' I said, facing her, my mouth thick with anger, 'do you realise how long it took Jeremy and me to do all this? To make Gresham Place what it is today?'

I remember her walking ahead of me, her silhouette etched against the encroaching darkness.

'You needn't worry on that score,' she said, her back to me. 'We'd look after it: the house the garden. You've done wonders, no-one can dispute that, but you're both growing old, and how long can you keep it all going? You're exhausted. I see you, hardly able to drag yourself around some days. As for Delia, well. Those scones of hers! And what a joke she looks in that costume, hobbling around with her teapot. Shut up shop, Harriet. Why don't you? Get him to take you away on a cruise, or something. He's a slave driver. It's time you stopped before you wear yourselves out.'

She emerged from the shadows then; a grey outline of a figure, stick in hand, right arm raised high above her head.

A sudden blow. A dull, chilling thud. Petronella staggered, half-turned and fell.

Delia placed her walking stick on the ground and stood, her body inclined as though in some grotesque prayer; stood stooped and motionless staring at the body lying curled and still.

I knelt and felt the slim bangled wrist. No pulse, no heart beat; hair sticky with blood and all the while the silent dark shadowed presence of Delia.

We buried Petronella. At least I did. Delia stood guard while I got to work, removing a foot or so of the top soil and placing it to one side before shovelling piles of red earth drenched and heavy. Breathing hard, the sweat pouring from me, my uttermost thought was to get finished before Jeremy returned. Dig, dig, dig. Rest. Dig, dig, dig. Rest. It was a shallow grave, about three feet in depth that was all I could manage, about three feet by six. When it was finished, I dragged the body from the rockery where she'd fallen, pulling it feet first into the hole. I would not, could not look at her and had to pretend she was some dead animal like a deer or calf. Afterwards, my hands sore and bleeding, I returned the soil, packing it down as much as I could, and spreading the left over earth about the bushes. Later, I would disguise the spot by planting a fast growing shrub, perhaps the small leafed, *Baggesen's Gold*, a plant that could be clipped neatly into shape. I tore branches from a nearby beech tree and lay them over the grave before returning to the house.

Delia had said nothing all this time and now the shock of what she had done hit her, as she clung to me helplessly, small whimpering sounds emitting from her lips.

It was getting late and I knew we must sort through Petronella's clothes, pack them away and store them in Delia's bedroom - Jeremy never went in there. Later, when he was out, we would light a bonfire. I scanned her wardrobe and the drawers under the bed. Jeans, a few tops, one or two frocks, a couple of jackets, silk scarves, shoes with impossibly high heels and a pair of trainers: these we dumped in large bin liners, clearing her dressing table of makeup and hunting for stray shoes under the bed. Then we heard his car. Jeremy was home.

My mind carnage, legs and arms weak to the point of collapse, I stumbled to my room, washed and combed my hair and breathless ran down the stairs to greet him. Standing in our hall, I told him Petronella had gone, taken her clothes and left without giving a forwarding address. I thought he might be angry with me for not trying to stop her but my news seemed to numb him and he stood by the front door confounded. He stared as though uncomprehending, first at me and then Delia who was sitting on the stairs, hugging her knees. Jeremy went pale and began to sway. When I went to him, touched his hand, it felt rigid and cold. It was probably this anguish of his that saved me from being further questioned.

Over the next few weeks he retreated into his art world, creating quick frantic paintings that I can only guess reflected his anger and loss. Later, as the days mimicked normality, he unburdened his grief. But it was to Delia he went. She reclaimed him, listening tirelessly to his outpourings, his laments; a clenched fist the only outward sign of her distress.

With Petronella gone they were friends again - bonded: the brother who had come to her aid, been her life-line all those years ago. There had been a car crash. He had urged her to hang on, to remain calm, as medics tried to free her from the mangled heap of metal. Afterwards, the doctors had to amputate her leg and Jeremy was there by her bedside, and later, it was Jeremy who protected her, imbued her with the confidence that neither parent could provide: parents who viewed their daughter's prosthesis as an indictment of their own making. It was only natural, that in time, after her husband deserted her, we should take her in, and offer her a home.

Our season continued, and whilst keeping a cautious eye on that tiny plot at the far end of the garden and planting my *Baggesen's Gold* I was relieved that this bushy addition scarcely raised comment from Jeremy who had lost all heart in the place. Delia now baked soft scones and hot tea with a smile on a face now astonishingly undimmed by any feelings of guilt. But there was no more dressing up. Jeremy returned his costume and never opened another poetry book.

Pets were not allowed at the house. A notice to that effect had been nailed to the side of the front door from the first day of opening.

I was showing a small group of visitors round the garden with its orange shrubs now bronzed with afternoon light: a retired clergyman, a school teacher, a couple of students and a female sculptor wearing a full length, blue woven cloak and a good deal of New Age jewelry. We had reached the water garden where the small group paused to admire our large selection of goldfish. Suddenly from out the folds of this woman's voluminous cloak, peeped a canine head. This was attached to a long white, short haired body now wriggling free of strong, fat arms. It shook itself then ran barking across the lawn trampling over the mauve and white autumn crocuses, past the low growing astors and golden rod, the clumps of yucca, towards the top of the garden, pausing now and then to sniff the rich damp earth. Now he was by the beech tree, his nose trailing the ground until he reached the grave.

'Stop! Stop!' I shouted running towards him. But his little feet were already clawing the mound, his long snout sniffing and ferreting.

I grabbed his collar. Too late. Petronella, her hand soiled and dry, and the arm, with the bangles rusted and split lay exposed on the surface. The sculptress was standing over me, just as Delia had done and when I lifted my head and looked into this woman's face it held horror and disbelief.

I was charged with the murder. But, of course, you know that too. Blood from my cut hand was found on a torn piece of tissue that I must have accidentally dropped into Petronella's grave. Careless! Careless! But when you are trying to do a dozen things at once, it is easy to overlook vital pointers.

Jeremy and Delia closed ranks, accusing me of insane jealousy and hatred. Delia died two weeks before the trial. Devious to the end.

Now that my prison sentence is completed, it is just Jeremy and me alone together in this house. Why do you stay? you may well ask. Habit perhaps? Or maybe I want to punish him with my presence: Harriet, the wife who murdered his one-time love.

How he must hate me as we face each other at meal times, silence our only companion, or when we pass each other on the stairs with eyes downcast.

But there was Ira. Ah Ira! After testifying at the trial, he left the country to live in Spain. He was the only one to speak highly of me - a good character testimony he gave me. Strange, when I had supposedly killed his girl friend. But I don't think there was much love lost between the two of them. If any. Ambition does not serve well as an aphrodisiac.

Now he is back. What a difference too: smartly dressed, and rich since inheriting the promised fortune that Petronella spoke of.

I have invited him to come and stay with us while he looks for a house. And why shouldn't I? This is my home after all, and I am entitled to have the final word.

Our house of course, is no longer open to the public; and besides Jeremy is getting very doddery and forgetful. Senile. He does as I say now and life is easier.

Ira and I have plans. We are thinking of going into the antique business together. And I must admit that we are developing an affection for each other. I won't go as far as to say it is love, but you never know. He is very attractive, even though he is years younger than I am, and in these enlightened times … well.

FAKING IT

It was Alec who brought up the subject of the painting.

'Should fetch a tidy sum at auction, old George should,' he said.

'Must we discuss this now? You know how I feel about it,' said Wanda, lighting up.

'I wish you hadn't Daddy,' chipped in Miranda, stirring her coffee, 'Not that one. We grew up with the old boy following us round the room with that "I know what you're up to" look.'

'Should be glad to be rid of it then,' retorted Alec. 'We need the cash, dear girl. The upkeep of this place is getting me down. Look at my shoes. No soles left.'

He raised his feet to show very sizeable holes in his country brogues.

Wanda blew a steady stream of smoke across the drawing room.

'You know that I'd give you the cash, if you'd only say. But you're too damned stubborn. That portrait's been in your family for yonks. I'm really quite peeved about it and you never asked me, your wife, just took it as read that you could sell it.'

'But Wanda, old duck. It was *my* great uncle not yours.'

'And a veritable dean he was too. We're a team, Alec, love. We do everything together. I'm quite upset.'

'Doing everything together, which we don't, does not warrant agreeing with everything. If you want to see me in the bankruptcy courts then fine.'

Wanda got up, and sniffing and coughing her way to the door, left the room.

Miranda and Richard exchanged looks, took the Scrabble board from under the table, laid out the pieces and asked me if I wanted to play.

'Thanks, I think I'll pass, if you don't mind,' I said, getting to my feet. 'Have an early night.'

It was the right move. Brother and sister looked relieved. They naturally wanted to be on their own to chew over the selling of a family heir loom; and of course I understood that but couldn't help feeling a pang of hurt as I walked through the hall to the stairs.

I was staying with The Gulley-Watsons while my new house was being built. The family were more my father's friends than mine. There was Wanda, a lean faced, tall woman who chain smoked, her husband who in the nineteen fifties could still go by the title of squire, and the twins who were in their twenties: A reasonably happy, clannish family, each going his or her own way; sometimes helping out in the small country parish, attending local dances at the village hall and church on Sundays where they sat in the privileged front pew.

Miranda, the daughter, was pretty - beautiful even, with long black hair that never lost its curl or shape even when wet. Her brother Richard was blonde, edgy with a temper but when his mood suited, possessed a sense of fun and a certain charm which he used intelligently to get his own way without appearing spoilt and unwieldy.

I was constantly aware of my place in the family. Certainly I was outside the group, not of it, however much they tried to welcome me and draw me in. It just didn't work for some reason. Not wanting to intrude, I'd go off for days at a time, sight-seeing, shopping, just killing time really. I was familiar with country-life, having been brought up in a similar village but I was unfamiliar at staying for lengthy periods as a guest in country houses. But when I suggested leaving they wouldn't hear of it. So there I was. Stuck.

The recent bother had gathered momentum before dinner. Everyone had been gathered in the drawing room for pre-prandial drinks. I noticed as I sat on the near threadbare Chippendale sofa, that an ancestral oil had been removed from the wall. The painting was of an old eighteenth century clergyman wearing his bands. His inscrutable gaze had fascinated me from the first moment I'd arrived at Chortlegate Manor.

'Where's the portrait?' I asked, putting both feet right in it.

The chatter ceased as the family looked at me in silence. I blushed. I must have seemed an intruder muscling in on something private; so I didn't pursue the subject and we finished our drinks just as Millie the housemaid called us in for dinner.

The meal went well enough although I sensed tensions. Wanda chatted away in her raspy voice about village events; Alec, reduced to grunts, drank rather too much claret; Miranda and Richard played their usual silly game of screwing bits of bread into small balls and rolling them across the table like marbles.

So now here I was, climbing the sweeping staircase to the panelled landing which led to my room. I opened my bedroom door, switched on the light and gasped. There it was - the portrait, lying face up on my bed.

For some moments I just stood there transfixed not quite believing what I saw. Then moving slowly to the bed I bent down and peered into the old man's lined face. He was well painted all right. There was something about the picture that drew you in: the texture, the brush strokes and of course, the clergyman's expression. But who'd put it on my bed and why? Had it been deliberately planted to implicate me in some sort of theft? Alec had taken it off the wall to sell. We all knew that. If I had stolen it then he couldn't sell it. No. That was a ridiculous notion. Perhaps he'd stored it somewhere safe prior to auction and Miranda or Richard had found it and placed it in my room … a ruse to prevent him from selling it or perhaps it was one of their stupid jokes.

I marched downstairs to the drawing room, my heart pounding, but Miranda and Richard must have changed their minds, for they'd already cleared away the Scrabble turned the lights off and left. Perhaps they knew I'd come looking for them.

Everywhere seemed suddenly quiet, unusually so: no movement, no sound, except for the ticking of the grandfather clock that stood just inside the front door.

I made my way back to my room, picked up the painting and placed it on the floor by the door before turning off the light and climbing into bed.

I was awakened at around two a.m. by the sound of heavy breathing. I froze - my heart in my mouth. Slowly, soundlessly, I edged myself onto my elbows and reached for the bedside light. I flicked on the switch just in time to see Alec tip-toeing to the door.

'What in heaven's name are you up to Alec?'

He swung round and looked at me sheepishly.

'So sorry my dear. Didn't mean to startle you. Hope you don't think that I was … ehm, well you know.

'No, I don't know,' I said, furiously drawing the sheet up under my chin.

'Just wanted old George back. Sorry to wake you, my dear.'

'But what's it doing in my room anyway? I thought you were going to sell it.'

'Not this one, dear.'

'What do you mean not this one?'

'This one's a copy. And I can assure you, it'll look every bit as good hanging in the drawing room as the original did. Now, no telling on me and Wanda won't know the difference. Promise?'

'Hang on Alec. She thinks you plan to sell the original.'

'Which I do. Which I shall. But she doesn't know for certain that I shall. When she sees this she will believe that I have decided to keep the picture to keep her happy. This will save a whole lot of agro. Believe me you don't want to witness Wanda having a real strop.'

'I see. Anything for a quiet life. But why hide the copy in here? Why not the attic or somewhere?'

'Because this is one of the safest rooms in the house. She never pokes her nose into guest rooms, when they're occupied. I'm so sorry about this, my dear. I tried to corner you earlier over sherry but the old girl's radar was on to me so I left it ... didn't get another chance, you see.'

'So you're definitely going ahead as planned then - selling I mean?'

'The original? You bet.'

'Where is it ... the original?'

'The safest place of all. The bank ... *my* bank. She can't get her mitts on it there.'

'Are you sure you're doing the right thing, Alec? It does seem rather dishonest.'

'The picture has to go, Jane. It's worth a great deal of money. It would break her heart to have to sell this place. The old girl's no money to speak of. Not nearly enough anyway.'

'But why is she so attached to the portrait? After all, the painting is of *your* uncle, not hers.'

'There's a certain sentiment attached to it, I'm afraid. It was painted by Roderick Whistlethorpe.'

'The famous seascape artist?'

'Not only seascapes. A lot of his income came from portraitures - commissions and such. Wanda, naughty girl, had an affair with him years back when she was single. He asked her to sit for him and it all snowballed from there. They were madly in love, according to her. They were all set to run away together but his wife found out and put the screws on.'

'I see.'

'As you probably know, he was killed during the war, poor chap. By then of course we were married and I had acquired my painting. Most of my uncle's assets came to me after he died. Uncle George never married you know. Just as well. That deanery of his was enough to freeze your balls off. Wanda won't know the difference. This copy's almost as good as the original; and it'll mollify the old duck to think that I have changed my mind in her interest.'

'But you're duping her Alec.'

'Needs must darling. Needs must. Now, while Wanda's snoring her head off, I'm going to tippy toe to the drawing room and hang this picture up. And a nice surprise for everyone tomorrow it will be. Want to come?'

'No thank you, Alec. I'm going back to sleep.'

'Oh come on! Have a nightcap - you'll sleep sounder with a brandy inside you.'

By now, of course, I was wide awake.

'Oh all right. If you insist.'

He gave me one of his charming grins.

'I do.'

A guilty sense of excitement replaced my annoyance as we crept downstairs like a couple of rogues with Alec clutching the picture under his arm.

Once in the drawing room he poured brandy for us both and then proceeded to hang the portrait back in the exact place of the original.

He stood back to admire. He paused, head on one side. Then his hands went up to his head and he groaned.

'What's the matter Alec?'

The frame - the ruddy frame - it's smaller than the original. It's left a mark - the old picture has left a dirty great sodding mark on the wallpaper.

On the right side of the portrait there was indeed a long dark dusty imprint where the original had hung. A shame. The actual copy was very good indeed.

'Who did you get to do it?' I asked. 'It's fantastic.'

'Better not tell.'

And he tapped his long insidious nose.

'Well, you'd better go into the kitchen and find some Ajax powder or something and see if you can get rid of the mark.'

Moments later he returned with a cleaning agent and cloth. He removed the picture and put it at his feet while he dabbed, prodded, and swore at the stain.

'Look at it! It's worse. It's rubbed the ruddy wallpaper off now.'

Sure enough, several of the pink roses were now minus their petals and there was an ugly grey water stain reaching the length of the picture frame.

'What are we to do?' Alec flung the cloth on the floor.

'You mean, what are *you* to do, Alec? This has nothing to do with me.'

'It was your idea to use the Ajax.'

'True. Have you got any spare wallpaper?'

But no sooner were the words out when the sound of footsteps stopped me in my tracks.

'Quick, hide,' cried Alec, dragging me towards a large corner cupboard. He flung open the door and ignoring my protests, pushed me inside and shut it tight.

'Hello darling,' I heard him say and peering through a chink, I saw Wanda, her wiry grey hair sticking out in all directions, dressing gown undone standing in what looked like men's slippers.

'What are you doing up at this hour, Alec?' she yawned. 'And what's that cleaning stuff doing here? It stinks. Have you spilt something?'

'Only a drop of brandy ... Couldn't sleep, came down, poured myself a stiffner and spilt some on the carpet.'

The cupboard was dusty, musty and dark. I felt my nose prickle - the prickly feeling grew worse until it exploded in one almighty sneeze. Wanda flung open the door her wrinkled eyes wide with amazement.

'Jane! What are you doing in the book cupboard?'

Taking the word 'book' as my cue I said that I was looking for one to read in bed.

'With the door shut?'

'I'm eh, I'm agoraphobic.'

'Agoraphobic? You never said.'

'Didn't I? Well, it's not something I generally talk about.'

'Where's your book then?'

'What? Oh yes. Sorry, I forgot.'

I turned back and saw to my horror that all the shelves were stacked to the gunnels with half rotten ancient volumes that must have been at least two hundred years old. I quickly chose one at random with half the pages missing and soggy with damp.

Wanda eyed me sharply but said no more on the subject. She turned to Alec who stood pinned against the wall.

'You've had a turn, haven't you? You're ill, aren't you? Come away from that wall now, there's a good chap.'

Alec nodded mutely but stood his ground.

'Come along now.'

He shook his head, and started biting his nails. I began to wonder if he was disturbed; that it was some family secret they hadn't told me about. Perhaps the picture on my bed and now hanging on the wall had been the real thing after all. Perhaps deep down he hadn't wanted to sell it and put it in my room pretending to himself that it was a copy. Who knew what his bizarre agenda might be.

I furtively made my way towards the door, but Wanda stopped me in my tracks.

'We've got to get Alec upstairs. Help me Jane.'

We took an arm each and pulled. But Alec wouldn't budge

'It's no good I'll have to call the doctor,' announced Wanda, making for the telephone on the far side of the room.

With her back now turned, Alec shook his head violently at me and mimed for me to pull out the socket. But where was it? I frantically looked along the skirting board and found it just feet away from Wanda who was standing by the French windows looking up the doctor's emergency number. In one swift movement I withdrew the plug just as she picked up the 'phone.

'The line's gone dead. It must be our trees caught up in the wires. What a damned nuisance!'

Now Miranda and Richard were standing there in their nightclothes demanding to know what was going on.

'Look! The picture's back,' yelled Miranda, eying it at Alec's feet.

'Don't you see mum, that's why he's in a state. He wants it gone, he wants to sell it, but it's back. By some miracle it's back. And then as an after-thought, 'So who the hell put it there?'

'No, that's not it at all,' argued Richard. 'Don't you see? Deep down, he loved old George so much, he just couldn't part with him. Poor old Dad. It's really sad. Look at him, he's heart-broken.'

The twins suddenly noticed me clutching my half rotten book, and asked what I was doing there.

'Jane couldn't sleep,' Wanda put in before I could answer, 'So she came downstairs to get something to read,' now feeling for a cigarette in her dressing gown pocket.

'From that old cupboard?' exclaimed Richard, eyeing me suspiciously. 'No-one ever gets a book out of that rotten old cupboard; they're all in Latin.'

'Never mind that,' snapped Wanda. 'The point is what are we to do with your father? He looks like an exhibit from *The Tate Britain*.'

'Daddy, can you hear us?' Miranda elocuted, putting her face up against his? And then turning to Richard, 'Do you think he's had a stroke? Perhaps we should take him to A and E.'

I stood on one foot and then the other debating what to do, whether to tell them the truth or try to get Alec out of his comatose state.

Then an idea struck. I slid out of the room while the family were all arguing; I ran into the kitchen to where the old servants' bells stood in a row, searched for the fire alarm and pressed it long and hard. I waited a few moments then ran into the hall where to my relief they had now all gathered, including Alec.

'Where's the fire, where's the fire?' everyone exclaimed and 'Where've you been Jane? Can you smell smoke?'

'Either there's a fire or someone pressed the bloody alarm,' cried Alec.

The shock hearing it go off seemed to have brought Alec to his senses. He appeared to have forgotten all about the picture and was now pacing the hall, the use of his legs and faculties generously returned to him.

'See anyone funny lurking about near the kitchen, Jane?' he barked, staring at me as though seeing me for the first time.

'No-one. I was in the loo.'

'Huh! Well, maybe there's an electrical fault, otherwise we'd all be charcoal by now.'

'There's no point in sending for the fire brigade if there's no fire,' put in Miranda.

'Well, we can't anyway, the phone line's dead,' said Wanda.

'Are you certain?' Richard asked. 'Let me check.'

'No!' I screamed, blocking the drawing room door.

'What's the matter with you?' Richard demanded. 'First we discover you're a Latin scholar and now you're hysterical. What's going on?'

'Nothing, nothing at all,' I quivered, worrying on Alec's behalf as well as my own. Who would hide the tell tale mark now, and how would I explain the unplugged phone? I felt displaced, guilty and miserable. How I longed for my house to be all ready and waiting for me to move into.

'Get away from that door Jane,' commanded Richard.' I want to go into the drawing room.'

'You can't!'

'Can't? Don't be ridiculous. What are you hiding in there?'

Why oh why didn't Alec help me? But Alec was walking around the hall sniffing for smoke.

Richard took hold of my shoulders and shoved me aside. He strode to the phone, tried it, saw the unplugged socket and turned on me.

'You did this, didn't you?'

'Did what?'

'Unplugged the phone. That's why you didn't want me to come in, wasn't it?'

'I don't know what you're talking about.'

'*Bellum domesticum*,' he yelled.

'What?'

'*Strife among family members.* Latin scholar indeed!'
'I never said I was a Latin scholar. *You* did.'
'Mother found you in the cupboard reading Latin text.'
'That doesn't make me a scholar.'
'Perhaps not which leads me to wonder what the hell you were doing there at all. I've never known anyone go into a cupboard to read, let alone shut the door.'

Tears burnt my eyes. I was about to weaken and blurt out the truth when there was the most almighty bang.

'Great God! Dad's shot himself,' cried Richard, rushing into the hall.

Standing in plus fours, his jaw slack with surprise whilst holding a smoking shot gun stood the game keeper; while crouched in the three corners of the hall cowered Wanda, Alec and Miranda.

'You bloody fool!' cried Alec snatching the gun. 'What's your game Hawkins? You could have slaughtered the lot of us.'

'Sorry, Sir, the thing went off in my hand, unexpected like.'

'You bloody idiot! Wasn't the safety catch on? Didn't you check the breech to see if it was loaded. I've a good mind to sack yeh. And what are you doing here anyway at this hour?'

'A poacher, Sir. Came to report him. Sorry Sir.'

'At this hour? We're in a family meeting Hawkins, can't it wait?'

'I've got him outside, Sir. Caught him red handed.'

Alec hesitated a moment as though remembering something.

'Oh very well,' he said at length, 'You'd better show him.'

'Shall he come through the front or the back Sir?'

'Well as we're all here and it's late or early, I'm not sure which, he'd better come through the front.'

Hawkins went out into the porch. 'You'd better come in Potter.'

There was a short pause before a small, wiry man wearing a tweed jacket, twill trousers and a shifty look, stepped inside. Alec blanched and for a moment I thought he was going to have another turn but he took hold of himself, told us all to go to bed then ushered the man at great speed into the study and shut the door.

'I only hope there are no hidden fires in the house, that's all,' said Wanda shedding cigarette ash onto the carpet as she went upstairs. 'Richard, before we bunk down for what's left of the night, check again, will you, all the rooms and the attic.'

She gave me a cursory nod and disappeared up one of the many corridors leading to the endless extensions that made the house rambling and architecturally shapeless.

I was now very chilled; with the central heating off the place was freezing, and I thought I'd have another nip of brandy before going back to bed.

Slipping once more into the drawing room I poured myself a good measure from one of the decanters on the sideboard, sat down in a high wing-backed chair and must have nodded off because the next thing I was woken by the sound of male voices outside the room. Downing the rest of my drink, and without time or opportunity to safely leave, I hid once more in the book cupboard.

Peeping through the same chink as before, I spied Alec standing in front of the picture with the poacher fellow at his side. 'Reckon you did a good job but look, it's not quite the same size as the original. Can you do something?'

'I'd have to take it with me,' said the poacher. 'Acquire a frame the exact match. Might be difficult. It'll cost.'

'No, no that's no good at all. I need it now. The old girl will twig when she sees that mark. And by the way, what were you doing in my woods at this unearthly hour?'

'Poaching,' like your game-keeper said. Caught a couple of nice rabbits too. Hope you don't mind, governor.'

'Don't have much option, do I?'

'That's right. Very true.'

'Look here, Potter. I've got to sell my original; but Wanda, being Wanda, will have a blue fit. That's why I must hang the copy here, for a quiet life, you understand?'

'This mark on the wall - we can get it off no probs.'

'But how?'

'Damp.'

'Damp?'

'That's what I said. Terrible thing is damp. It can strike any time, can damp.'

'But it doesn't look anything like damp.'

'Not yet it doesn't but by the time I've finished with it ...'

I leant exhausted against one of the shelves. Before I knew it, books were careering down on my head.

Alec flung open the cupboard door. 'Oh, it's you again. More Latin reads?'

Potter picked up a couple of the books that had fallen.

'What have we here? Oh yes, very nice: Mould, mildew and stink ... perfect damp components. Problem solved.'

'I don't quite see,' began Alec. 'We've plenty of damp here - and being surrounded by so many trees doesn't help.

'Condensation, rain, penetration and rising damp - oh dear, oh dear. What a shame, but there, that's old buildings for you.'

'My dear fellow ...' broke in Alec. 'I don't quite get your point.'

'It's simple. We rub this fungal stuff from these 'ere pages over the walls, where the picture had hung and over that wet 'orrible mark you made. And there you have it - damp. When the misses comes down tomorrow and sees it, you just tell 'er the damp's got in. Tell 'er it's lucky for all of you that the picture's still in good nick.

'Why, yes. It's worth a try Potter.'

Alec grinned at me as though the whole thing had been my idea, which was sweet of him, and they set to work shaking out several of the loose, soggy pages and smearing them on the wall to cover the marks with more authentic ones.

'C'or what a pong,' said Potter, slapping more paper over the wet. 'Better do a bit more somewhere else to make it seem a real big problem, don't you agree governor?'

And so there we were smearing walls at three a.m. with me sneezing away and Potter taking nips of brandy now and then to fortify himself.

The next day, true to his word, Wanda was none the wiser. She tut-tutted over the sudden outbreak of damp in their 'one good room' but kissed and praised Alec for his wisdom in changing his mind and keeping the portrait. She was completely taken in and refrained from asking what they were to do for money, presumably not wanting to rock the boat.

Richard had calmed down and was back to his old self while Miranda kept patting her father's head and telling him he was the best dad in the world. As for me? Well, I smiled my way through breakfast, thanked them profusely for their hospitality at lunch, presented Wanda with a large box of handmade chocolates, accepted Miranda's offer of a lift to the nearest train station and left for Devon early evening.

There's a very reasonable small hotel on the edge of Dartmoor. All the bedrooms have locks; it's modern with all mod cons and best of all, it's completely damp free. I think I'll stay there until my house is ready.

HOME IS WHERE THE HEART IS

A pool of water stands between us ... small, transparent and round.

I stare. He stares.

'We should have had a survey done. We should.'

'We decided to skip the survey, remember? A bargain like this doesn't come along every day. Fetch a bucket, Anne.'

'We haven't got a bucket.'

'The washing up bowl then.'

He's snappy now, leaning across me to get to the sink.

'Shall I ring for a plumber?' I offer.

'Do you know a plumber, Anne?'

'Not personally, no. But there's *Yellow Pages*.'

'You don't know who you'll get from *Yellow Pages*.'

He takes a J. Cloth, and begins mopping up a small trickle ... river sounds too dramatic, that has suddenly appeared from nowhere.'

'It's coming from under the floorboards now,' I squeak.

'Well, go on then, get *The Yellow Pages*.'

'Oh, but I thought you said ... Do you know where it is?'

I'm in the hall now which is several degrees above freezing.

'Search me. You packed the books and stuff.'

I glance at the unlabelled packing cases lined up against the wall.

'I think I must have thrown out *The Yellow Pages*.'

'You throw out everything, Anne. You'll throw the cat out next.'

My heart gives a sudden lurch. The cat! Where's the cat? I've forgotten the cat. I let out a strangled cry, rush back to the kitchen to confess my latest sin to my husband who wears a look of thunder that stretches from brow to beard.

'Gerald!' I quake.

'Gerald?'

'I think I forgot to pack the cat. I must have left him behind at our old house. What shall I do?'

The puddle of water is now a large puddle of water and the trickle from nowhere is now a definite river flowing nicely towards the hall. But to me this is nothing compared to what I've done. The couple who've bought our old house, hate cats. Mr McTooth is allergic to cat's fur and Mrs McTooth has a Rottweiler called Fritz, who will probably tear poor Gerald to bits.

I burst into tears and Tom tut tuts and asks if I know where the mains water tap is.

'I don't,' I sniff. 'I must go back and fetch Gerald.'

'From Fife?' he storms. 'You plan to travel four hundred and sixty miles to Fife from Surbiton for a mangy cat that should have been castrated years ago.

I stare.

'Well, off you go then.'

Biting my lips, I watch him wring out the cloth for the umpteenth time.

'What are you waiting for, Anne? Don't mind me. Don't mind this river that we are soon to enjoy a swim in.'

'Stop shouting, Tom!'

'We've got to switch this water off at the mains. Then fetch a plumber. It would be extremely helpful, therefore, if you were to look for the mains water tap instead of carping on about that creature with the sly eyes and the wobbly walk.'

'He hasn't got a wobbly walk. He fell out of a tree; he's just a little lame that's all. And his eyes are lovely.'

Tom gives me a hard look. I recall the early looks he gave me and they are not the same looks at all. Gone are the seductive brown eyes, gone are the full sensual lips and the half-smile that promised a night of unforgettable sex. I'm face to face with a monster, whose temper would scare the very snakes off Medusa's scaly head.

I slink off to look for the said tap in this Victorian house that has no damp course, a leaky roof and a potential demolition order hanging over it. The rooms are high ceilinged, bare, with no sign of anything apart from peeling paper and mushroom-like growths sprouting out of various corners. But a mains tap? How am I to face my once sweet natured husband, who may, as I speak, be removing his shoes and socks and paddling in two feet of water?

A purring sound stops me in my tracks. It's coming from the bathroom with its ancient water closet and chipped bath.

I open the door, turn on the light and there he is: Gerald sitting unconcerned by the wall. Oh joy! Then I remember. I packed him along with the Yellow Pages in the cane laundry basket. And there's the laundry basket next to the lavatory - Where I put it - and there is the Yellow Pages and there is Gerald.

I lift him into my arms and notice sticking out of the wall, and covered in old sacking, what looks like a mains water tap.

'I've found them!' I yell. 'All of them!'

My excited voice echoes round this impossible house, a house that I know, despite this, that and the other I already love.

UNDELIVERED

The present, small and neat, lay unopened on the sitting room floor. It had lain there for a whole week. When it rained and Benjamin was bored he would kick it about a bit.

'Don't do that,' his mother would say, a small smile edging her lips.

'Why don't you open it then mummy?'

'Because it isn't mine to open Benjamin.'

'Can *I* open it?' he asked, and picked it up and gave it a shake.

'No. It isn't yours either. We must save it for Auntie Hester.' And she took her duster and rubbed away at a water mark on a little side table.

Benjamin climbed onto a chair and dive-bombed the parcel over mummy's head.

'I want to open it. Please! Please!'

Mummy snatched it from his hands and placed it firmly on the sideboard. 'I said no.'

'Then *you* open it. Auntie Hester wouldn't mind.'

'We don't open other people's things.'

'You opened my Daddy's letter to Auntie Hester. I saw you.'

'That was different.'

'Why? Why was it different?'

'Because it was. Now go and play.'

Benjamin stared hard at mummy. 'Why did you cry when you read the letter?'

'I said go and play!'

Benjamin dragged his toy box out of the cupboard. 'I think you like me kicking the parcel around the floor.'

'No, I don't. I like you kicking your ball outside in the garden.'

'Then why did you leave it on the floor?'

'It takes up less space,' said mummy flicking her duster back and forth.

'It's quite small mummy. Small parcels don't take up much space.'

'Go and play.'

'What do you think is inside the parcel mummy?'

'I don't know and I don't care.'

'Then why have you gone red?'

'I'm hot. Go away!'

And all this time the parcel shone small and golden in its wrapping paper.

Benjamin searched amongst his toys for some lego pieces. 'When will Auntie Hester come to pick it up mummy?'

'Soon.'

'How soon is soon?'

But mummy, now busy dusting the mantelpiece did not answer.

'When is daddy coming home?'

'I don't know Benjamin.'

'I miss daddy.'

Mummy's duster fell from her hand. 'Yes, darling, I know. We both miss him.'

'Will Daddy come for the present?'

'I don't know darling.'

'Why didn't Daddy take it with him when he left us?'

'He forgot, I expect. He was very busy packing.'

'Will Auntie Hester come and visit us, mummy?'

'I don't know.'

'If Daddy comes for the parcel she won't need to visit us. I miss Auntie Hester.'

Mummy stroked his blonde hair and kissed his forehead.

'She plays snakes and ladders with me. And she laughs a lot. Auntie Hester is very pretty mummy.'

'Yes. Oh yes she is.'

'I want to take the parcel to her. I want to give Auntie Hester her present.'

'Do you Benjamin?'

'Yes. She would like that. She would give me those biscuits with the pink icing sugar on top. I love Auntie Hester Mummy. Please can we go and see her?'

Mummy stopped dusting, picked up the parcel and thrust it into Benjamin's hands.

'Open it!' she demanded, her voice suddenly cross.

Benjamin looked up from his lego. 'But you don't want me to open it. You said.'

'I've changed my mind.'

'Why? Why have you changed your mind?'

'Because the longer it stays here the longer I think of daddy.'

'I think that parcel makes you sad.' And Benjamin left his half-made Batman on the floor and flung his arms around mummy's knees.

'So open it Benjamin, please!'

He thought very hard. What should he do? First mummy said no and now she said yes. That didn't make sense. It was like wanting sticky toffee so much and mummy saying no and then her giving him the full bag to guzzle all up.

'No!' he said standing up straight. 'I won't open the parcel.'

'Please,' said mummy. I want to see what's inside.'

'I said no!'

'But *you* wanted to see what was inside … didn't you?' she added hotly and began to dust the furniture all over again.

'Yes I did.'

'Well then … open it Benjamin.'

'No! I won't!'

'Do as you're told!' And mummy stamped her foot and threw her cloth on the floor.

'Get on with your dusting mummy.'

'I've finished my dusting.'

'Then go and play on your mobile.'

'Don't tell me what to do Benjamin.'

'You tell me what to do all the time.'

'That's different.' And mummy ran from the room and slammed the door behind her.

Benjamin stared at the parcel. He picked it up and shook it. It rattled. But instead of wanting so badly to open it, he felt a lump rise in his throat. By swallowing very hard he could just stop the tears falling down his cheek. He knew that now more than ever before he had to be brave. There was something in that parcel that made mummy sad, made her want to cry. Perhaps if Auntie Hester was given daddy's present it would make Auntie Hester sad too.

Benjamin didn't want to kick the thing about any more. He didn't want to play ball with it or to open it. Most of all he didn't want Auntie Hester to have it. Something had to be done but what?

He tidied up all his lego and returned the pieces to his toy box, all the while trying to work out what to do. Mummy wouldn't allow him to visit Auntie Hester or daddy, so what was he to do? And then he had the idea. He would bury it. He would bury the present in the back garden. If it was deep in a hole, no-one would see it, and no-one would find it. It would be out of sight forever. And Daddy couldn't hurt any of them ever again.

Benjamin carried the parcel outside, found a trowel in the shed, dug a hole next to a white rose bush and threw it in. He spread soil over the top so that none of the shiny bits showed.

The lump in his throat had gone and he did not feel like crying anymore. Instead he found his football. It was hidden deep amongst the laurels. He picked it up, walked onto the lawn and kicked it extra hard all over the garden.

Mummy played on her mobile. Daddy stayed away. And Auntie Hester, who knew nothing of her present, remained none the wiser.

FROZEN IN TIME

Last Thursday I drenched my shopping list: The sprouts ran into the toilet rolls and the mushroom soup into a packet of aspirin. I took a screwed up tissue from my sleeve and mopped up, but the little nouns awash with my salty tears, were now illegible. So I screwed up the paper and pushed it behind two packets of ginger nuts. Biscuits were not on my list. This aisle, this sea of goodies I try to avoid when I shop.

Last week my husband left me another kind of note unblemished by tears; and to add insult to injury we were flooded out. Literally. Now the cob walls cried. The stream outside our thatched cottage had burst its banks filling our garden and turning it a murky brown; drenching the roses and frightening Monty our Cairn, who ran inside for shelter.

She called then ... my glamorous neighbour Estelle.

I was filling buckets with filthy sludge as she sloshed through the wet in yellow wellies.

'Where's Rab?' It was more of a demand than a question. There was no, 'Can I help?' Just, 'Where's Rab?'

I wanted to throw the bucket of water in her face. But didn't. I wanted to stick her head under the murky pool slopping around our feet. But didn't. I wanted to take off my *Marks and Spencer's* scarf and wind it tight around her neck. But I didn't do that either.

Instead I told her politely, that he was on emergency duty with the fire brigade.

I knew this would frustrate her need, her hunger to lay those limpid brown eyes on him. She wanted to insist, as though that might bring him back the sooner. But she's afraid of giving herself away. Stupid woman! Doesn't she know that I know? That his note left under the telephone gave me the facts: Always a great one for facts my husband: ex-military, you know.

So there we stood ... she, me and the filthy water swirling around our ankles. Neither of us moved. We just stared at one another eye to eye unblinking like a couple of rabbits transfixed under the headlights of a car.

And it was then, caught in the moment, that I wondered if Rab would really leave me and go to her. Or would I leave Rab? Would I perhaps, on a sudden hostile whim, murder Estelle? Would she murder me? Life would be so much easier, so much less complicated if one could simply allow time to stand still. Stand and stare. Stare and stand. So many twists along life's journey; so many variations to explore and ponder:

Perhaps the heavens might open again and wash us down the lane; Estelle and I screaming with fear and indignation. Or Rab return and make things all right between us. Perhaps he would take off to the Bahamas never to be seen again: Or maybe Monty would bite Estelle on the knee and she would die of lockjaw; or I might fall in love with the man who would come to repair the drains. If fate existed, and who's to say it doesn't, how much easier life would be. None of us would hold any responsibility for anything that we did, but glide from one event to the next - Hapless.

It was Estelle who finally broke the gaze, who turned and with one of her silly little waves paddled back down the garden path to her super deluxe modern property. She and Des seem to have avoided this deluge of water, since their house was built on top of a hill.

And the outcome of all this? Well, Rab completed his shift and came home; I tore up his note, saying that everything on the telephone table had been soaked through and so it was illegible. And now, as I sit here talking to myself, one month has past. For all I know the affair is still going on. I've said nothing. Neither has he. Why not? Well, the answer's simple. I hate scenes, so does Rab - hence his note. That he didn't inquire as to my having read it, tells me that he is content to let sleeping dogs lie.

Estelle hates scenes too. Isn't that an odd coincidence? And in all fairness it has to be said that she does give the most superb dinner parties, and more importantly, owns the most divine and enviable jewellery. Add to this my garden and thatched cottage with its Elizabethan inglenook fireplace and … Well, why change all that? Why give it all up? Better to own one's thoughts, pure or otherwise and keep quiet. Why confront and radically move on? Some of us are better at coping with skeletons in cupboards than others.

Oh, didn't I tell you about mine? That really is remiss of me.

My skeleton is hidden away - very cleverly, very neatly in an old cornflakes' packet. No-one would think of looking there, would they? It makes me smile sometimes to think that such an exquisite, expensive item lies buried beneath some silly old wheat flakes.

But every so often when Rab goes out, probably to meet his mistress, I'm irrevocably drawn towards it. I pour myself a large glass of wine, or better still a gin and tonic; take the cornflake packet down from the kitchen shelf, one we never use, walk upstairs and sit at my dressing table. Taking my time, treasuring the moment, I stare at the packet, rather like the way I stared at Estelle but my thoughts are very different. My heart hammers away as slowly, oh so slowly, I open it and lift out a single string of the most beautiful pearls you have ever seen. I gaze at their luminosity; those handsome rich gleaming orbs resting in my hand.

I caress and clasp them to me like a lover, before placing them around my neck and fastening the diamond clasp. Click! Each little pearl mine ... imprisoned, captured around my neck. Sitting back in my velvet chair I am entranced.

She misses them, of course she does. Who wouldn't? But the insurance people will pay up, and I doubt that the police will find out who did it. Well, naturally we would be the last suspects on their list. After all we are such good, honest neighbours.